T0077602

A Moment

A Moment

Of Love, Friendship and Family

Purva Gole

PARTRIDGE

Copyright © 2016 by Purva Gole.

ISBN: Softcover   978-1-4828-7158-6
            eBook   978-1-4828-7159-3

All rights reserved. No part of this book may be used or reproduced by any means, graphic, electronic, or mechanical, including photocopying, recording, taping or by any information storage retrieval system without the written permission of the author except in the case of brief quotations embodied in critical articles and reviews.

Because of the dynamic nature of the Internet, any web addresses or links contained in this book may have changed since publication and may no longer be valid. The views expressed in this work are solely those of the author and do not necessarily reflect the views of the publisher, and the publisher hereby disclaims any responsibility for them.

Print information available on the last page.

To order additional copies of this book, contact
Partridge India
000 800 10062 62
orders.india@partridgepublishing.com

www.partridgepublishing.com/india

Contents

To the young people
Who have fallen in Love,
To the people who believe in Love,
To the people whom I have been loving.

Acknowledgment

Dear reader,

Thank you for choosing *A Moment…* and giving a chance to a young writer in me. As I was penning this book, I lived every character of the story. And these characters taught me a lot. Really, in this process I have changed. From a chirpy carefree girl I have grown reflective and mindful.

Dearest Mom and Dad, I am privileged to have you in my life. I can't thank you as gratitude is a small measure for what you mean to me. Without your motivation and encouragement this literary journey would never be complete. Mom, thanks for inspiring me every day, at every moment to turn this dream into reality. Dad, you have always been my super hero, your optimistic attitude has surely helped. How can I ever forget my inspiration, my best friend – My Sister. You were always there besides me, supporting me and guiding me all through the way. The days when I was down you were there to bring me up and bring a smile on my face. Actually you are my support system. Yes seriously I am blessed with the best.

Thanks a lot to the entire team of Partridge India.

My humble work is a tribute and token of appreciation to my guru- my teacher. Thank you Rajnikant sir for the tremendous support you have given to me, and motivating me with words of encouragement and believing in my talent. Thanks Aditya for being my first reader.

And yes if I don't thank them they all will surely kill me for it. Thanks a lot my buddies- Namrata, Priyanka, Hetvi, Yakshita, and Kashyapi. Thanks for never letting the smile on my face fade away by your P.J's, for teasing me every now and then and sizzling up my life with verve and vibrancy! Love you gals a lot.

And lastly thanks to all well wishers who have been a part of this phase and will continue to wish well for me. Happy reading.

Prologue

On a breezy day, my sister and I were walking on the streets of Cambridge. We had been walking for so long now, I was beginning to get tired and we decided to grab a coffee at Starbucks. Mom had just called asking us to bring her some stuff she needed and we decided that my sister would go buy the things while I wait for her at the Starbucks. She walked out and I got into the queue to get my beverage. There he was. The most amazing guy I had ever seen. He looked Indian, the complete personification of the tall, dark and handsome cliché. Dress in a green t- shirt and jeans, and Reebok shoes, he seemed just a little younger than my sister. "One coffee wrap please", he ordered. "$4.25, sir" He handed a $5 bill to the guy at the counter. "Sorry sir we don't have change," was the prompt response. He checked his wallet, he didn't have any change himself, just two $2 notes and a $5 note.

Before I could think, I blurted out "Would you have $4?" I guess my mind had just spontaneously decided to help him, as if it was the most important thing to do.

"Yes, but…"

"Give it to the guy, I have 25 cents here."

"No, its fine; I hardly know you."

"When people meet for the first time they are strangers."

"What?"

"Nothing. You, Indian?"

"Yes"

"Me too. That makes us strangers no more. Now would you take 25 cents from me?"

"Ok, I'll take them but will pay you back one day."

"Yeah sure, that's ok."

He paid the money and went aside waiting for his coffee to arrive. It was my turn to order coffee now. I placed and took my order and was making my way to a table.

"You gave me 25 cents; I could at least give you company for some time."

"Sure why not." We settled into a cozy table for two.

"So we share a table and yet we don't even know each other's name. Funny, isn't it?"

"Oh! I am Aditya Patel. I am an engineering student, studying at Massachusetts Institute of Technology."

"Wow! Have heard a lot about the place. I am Purva and I am in high school."

"I thought so, you look quite young..."

"So, where are you from in India?"

"I am from Vadodara, Gujarat."

"You gotta be kidding me, I am also from Vadodara!"

"What a coincidence! Two people from the same city came all the way to Cambridge to meet accidentally! So how are you here?"

"Well I am an aspiring writer. I have come here to find a story."

"Oh really are you a writer? You are quite young still."

"Well the first part was true, I am a writer but I have not come here to find a story or something. I have come here with my family to attend my cousin's wedding. My uncle is a professor in one of the universities. My sister has gone out for some work so I am waiting here for her. I have written some poetry and some romantic short stories."

"Romantic stories! Good God! You are full of surprises!"

I thought I was imagining and wasn't sure if he had really emphasized on the word romantic.

"Yes..."

"So you believe in love and all that stuff?"

"Yes, of course! Who doesn't?"

"You teenagers can be such emotional fools sometimes. Wake up, man! There is nothing like love in this world. It's all fake."

"You sound like a 70 year old."

"You won't understand. You are too young for it. You have not seen the real world and are still living in your own fairytale world."

"Let me guess... Did you recently break up with your girlfriend? Did she leave you? That's what is hurting you and depressing you out. Correct me, if I am wrong"

"No, it's nothing like that," he replied bluntly.

"Please, you don't need to lie about this. You have break-up written all over you."

"Alright. Fine. Yes, I had a break up. It's all over now. And my whole experience has assured me that love does not exist"

"See I told you. One break up and everything is over. I mean you are talking as if you are going to die tomorrow. Life is too long, buddy, and one couldn't spend it all alone. Everyone needs someone - a shoulder to cry, someone to love. Maybe you quit too early..."

"Don't say anything if you don't know what the matter was. I have put a lot of efforts to save our relationship."

"Who said I am talking about your relationship? I was trying to say that you should not quit on life. One break up is not more important than a whole lifetime. If love is not there, life isn't worth living. What if a stupid, idiot, useless person ditched you..."

"Aditi was not like that, ok?"

"So, it's someone called Aditi... See this trick never fails. Guess you still love her, or you wouldn't defend her."

"You've told so much, a little more couldn't hurt. what's your story? Cut the suspense!"

"Why should I tell you my story? How can I trust writers? They are always in search of a story. Who knows if you take my story, publish it and earn money? And I still hardly know you.

"Well if you tell me your story and if I publish it I will earn fame. That way you could help me realize my dearest dream. Helping someone isn't a bad idea, is it? You know, someone rightly said that your secrets are the safest with strangers, as strangers disappear and the secret goes with them."

"You are really stubborn. And you sound more sensible than your age."

"I have heard that often, however, I would still take that as a compliment. Now can we focus on your story?"

"Why would you be so interested in my story?"

"I just am. I could tell you more once I hear the story, so stop questioning. You are testing my patience now."

"Alright, But I am a bit lost, don't know where to start."

"Well, let's just start from the very beginning."

He started his story… and took me to a journey of dreams, a journey of friendship, a journey of love….

1

New Beginnings

"Wake up Adi….you are late again…"

My morning started with the piercing voice of my mom, making me literally jump off my bed. I was late, as usually is the case. Mom handed me a cup of coffee that I drank, standing in the balcony. I could smell the fresh air of the early morning and hear the chirping of birds. The sun was slowly trying to come out of the cage of the clouds as its light rays began peeping through the spaces; wanting to start a new story, a new chapter, writing a new page of life. I was in the city of art, the city with banyan trees, a city with a heart as huge as its landmark - the Lakshmi Vilas Palace – Vadodara. Vadodara is said to be the city of small spaces but large dreams. There is nothing distinctly extraordinary in the city but the city itself is extraordinary. Most of the people will complain about the lack of a happening nightlife in the city but I would say that the city is safer than any other city of India, whose beauty lies in its simplicity. I was getting late for school, so I got ready to go to school in just five minutes. I was unable to complete my breakfast which always makes mom cross, it's become a habit with me these days.

My mom - Falguni Patel's thoughts were not so old-fashioned like her name. She meant everything to me. Her whole world

1

revolved around me so sometimes she would become over-protective, which is the exact motherly thing that moms do.

My dad passed away when I was just 4 years old. I was too young then to have any memories with him. With dad gone, money was always a matter of struggle for the family. Mom decided to save as much as we could, so she could provide for my education. Mom was a primary school teacher and earned barely Rs.5,000 a month, which was barely enough to meet all the expenses of the family.

In spite of being late that day, I miraculously managed to reach my class 2 minutes early. As I was stepping inside, I saw the board that was hung there. It said - "12 SCI". I felt a feeling of pride as I read that. It was a dream come true...

It was the first day of school after the holidays. I was excited and nervous, as in one more year my life would change. I entered the class to find the same faces, everyone sitting in the same way as they used a year ago - the carefree students sitting on the last bench, the average students in the middle, the nerds of the class (including me) on the first benches. I would always sit next to Krishnanath, the topper of our class. He would always be engrossed in his books, so much so that, even after five years of sitting next to him, we were yet to have a proper conversation. Lost in my thoughts, I missed noticing that Mrs. Mitra, our teacher, had already entered the class.

"ADITYA PATEL, what are you looking at? Sit down please", she shouted. This would perhaps be the first time Mrs. Mitra was angry with me.

I had just taken my seat when I heard someone... "May I come in."

I turned to the door to see who it was and there stood a tall, charming, confident girl with long, wavy hair. Her dark brown eyes were full of pride; she seemed intelligent. She wore the same school uniform that we all did, yet she looked so different from others. Meanwhile, Mrs. Mitra welcomed her into the class.

"Attention students. She is Aditi Sharma. She has joined this year."

As luck would have it, Krishnanath had gone to bring Mrs. Mitra's books for the class, so she came and sat in the vacant seat next to me. That one moment seemed absolutely magical, as if God was being kind to me that day. Maybe if I had wished for something else, I would have got it as well!

She was a complete stranger to me, yet she looked familiar. While I was celebrating the moment in my head, Krishnanath came back and looked extremely pissed, it was an expression I couldn't completely comprehend, but I figured it had to do with his favorite seat being taken by someone else. He took the seat behind me. He continued to glare at me, and I had to just ignore him.

I tried to focus in the class, but with such a beautiful girl sitting next to you, it is not quite the easiest thing to do, especially when you have boring Mrs. Mitra talking boring physics concepts in front of you. But I didn't really have a choice here, I couldn't keep staring at her, I needed to focus on what Mrs. Mitra was saying. The day passed without any further events and I went home.

That night as I lied down with my head in my mom's lap, I was preoccupied with the events of the morning. I found myself still thinking about Aditi. I kept wondering what her first thoughts would have been about me, did she even notice me…I lost track of time and fell asleep in the same lost state.

The next day, surprisingly, I managed to reach school well before time. I was still lost in my own thoughts. Aditi was there, and she took the seat next to me like the previous day. She didn't yet know that it was Krishnanath's seat. I prayed that Krishnanath would give let her be and give his seat to her.

Thought I wanted it to happen, I wasn't really expecting Aditi to strike a conversation with me. But that's exactly what happened and it took me by surprise.

"Hi Aditya I am Aditi. I have come from St. Xaveries School."

After a long pause I replied and managed to mutter "hi".

"I think you are a person of very few words!"

She had the complete wrong idea about me! I was never a person of few words!

I replied, "No I am not like that, why do you think so?"

"Yesterday you didn't speak a single word, so I just guessed. I thought you are the intelligent-types, engrossed in books all the time. You were so lost all day!"

Little did she know that it was the best I could do to avoid staring at her.

To cover-up everything I said, "It's nothing like that, I just got a little tensed as it's our class 12..."

"Oh don't worry; you have the whole year to take tension. Calm down and everything would be alright."

This was just making me nervous, so I decided to change the topic. "Yeah sure. Well, you are not a Gujarati, so where're you from?"

"I was born in Mumbai. Years ago, my grandfather established his business here. I was barely two years old then."

She had opened her books and had stopped looking at me, but I couldn't take my eyes off her just yet. The bell rang just then and the classes began. It was just another day at school. The next two periods went a bit normal as I tried my best to focus on what the teacher was explaining.

Up until then, love was something I had read about in books and seen in the movies. With the limited knowledge and no experience that I had, I had perhaps made up my mind that love at first sight was unreal and it happened only to fools. Today it seemed, I was becoming one of those fools myself.

Two classes later it was Physics class and Mrs. Mitra gave shocked us by saying that she would be giving a test tomorrow. This scared Aditi more than it scared me.

"Oh no! Today I have to study physics that is really not my cup of tea", she said.

"Don't worry. Someone told me this morning that we had a whole year to worry…"

"Yeah right. I have a phobia for physics! It is the scariest subject ever!"

"Chill. We can study together, if it's ok with you. I am good with Physics, I could help you. And you seem good with Chemistry which isn't really my cup of tea, so you could help me with that."

After thinking for a while, she said "Ok"

It felt no less than winning a Gold at the Olympics! She said yes!

"Ok, let's meet at 7?"

"Sure! Let's meet at the coffee shop near the school.

"Cool. Not a problem."

2

Love at first sight. Really?

There started our daily meetings. I would religiously reach the coffee shop five minutes before 7, and Aditi would always be ten minutes late. For the first few minutes I would do nothing but keep looking at her and day-dream. Then, I would try and concentrate on physics.

"Sometimes, you really get lost...", she would complain.

"Maybe I was lost in solving the numerical."

I enjoyed her company a lot. And thanks to her, I started enjoying physics and chemistry too.

Three months down the line, I was now a good friends with Aditi, at least a good study buddy. We hardly talked much besides studies.

One night, I was just about calling it a day and going to sleep when my phone rang. It was our third semester Physics board exam the next day and I had been studying till 1:00 am. I was surprised, there was nobody who called me that late. The name that flashed on my phone was none other than Aditi, that surprised me even more. I was worried that if she was alright.

"Aditi are you alright, is everything ok?" I even forgot to say hello!

"Yes, Aditya all is fine. Why do you sound so worried?"

"It's nothing. You called me so late so I just thought…"

"Do I need to be in some trouble to be able to call you this late?"

"It isn't like that. You can call me anytime you want. You are a friend after all, right?"

"Yes of course. You just made me forget why I had called you."

"Oh sorry, yes, please tell me what happened"

She turned a few pages of the textbook and said, "Could you open your physics text book to page number 33 and explain the example 13."

I began searching for the textbook and said, "Aditi, you know tomorrow is our exam and it's 1AM, right? I am sorry but you are asking me to solve this big numerical at way past midnight!!!"

I was kidding, for sure! And as always, she took it seriously!

"You called me your friend right, so time to prove it"

"Alright, alright, I was just kidding!"

"That's ok, now could you explain it quick, I would like to go to sleep."

"It will take a little time to figure it out. I will solve it and forward the solution to you on WhatsApp, would that be alright?"

"Cool, not a problem."

"Bye, good night. I think we will meet after the exam now, as our examination seats are different."

In a very sleepy tone she said, "Yeah sure I will text you when we can meet to prepare for the next exam. Bye!"

Something was different in Aditi's tone. And it was good. She had never been so friendly before. Maybe, I was as important to her as she was for me. It was my assumption, but it felt good to think about. I was happy and satisfied that at least I was her good friend.

The next day my exam went great. I waited for a while but Aditi neither texted me nor called me. I decided to call her.

I dialed her number and as soon as she picked up, she said, "Sorry, sorry, sorry I know I had to call but I was stuck in some work so could not call you. I am really very sorry…"

"It's fine Aditi… Chill…"

"Yes Mr. Right."

"Ok so jokes apart, we need to study, exams are not over yet!"

"Yes I know, I am bored of studying! I don't know how I would be able to keep up once the Board exams start."

"There is a lot of time for boards, Aditi, first let us think about today"

"What is there to think? We are meeting at the coffee shop, I will let you know the time."

"Actually, I was thinking something else…"

"Oh! What's cooking in the scholar's mind?"

"You could come to my place to study, you know? There will be less distractions and no noise like there is in the coffee shop."

I wanted mom to meet Aditi. I had no secrets from mom. Aditi and I had nothing going between us, but I still wanted mom to meet her. Moreover, it was getting a little too much economically to be at the coffee shop every day, my pocket money couldn't take the daily hit, even though we had played dutch all the time.

"Aditya, I am ok with coming to your place, I just thought your mom wouldn't like it so I never insisted." I was so relieved, "I had never asked you about it because I thought it might be too far for you"

"Nope, it's totally fine. I will be there in half an hour."

"Cool. No problem"

3

Friendship is love

I was really very excited but I forgot to ask mom if it was alright to invite Aditi home. I rushed to her as soon as I could. I had not talked to her since I had come home after giving the exam.

As I entered her room she said, "So now you got time to meet your mother!" "Sorry mom, I was on a call"

"Yes, I am observing Adi, since past few days you are spending a lot of time on the phone, what's the matter with you?"

"Mom it's nothing like that", I said keeping my head in her lap.

"So then, tell me how it is", she asked curiously.

"Mom I have a new special friend."

"Oh! Someone special! My little Adi has grown up now! Who is she? Tell me."

I was blushing red…

"Mom, her name is Aditi, Aditi Sharma. She is my classmate. We have been studying together for three months now. I don't know much about her family but she is a good person. I think you will also like her when you will meet her. She is so free, brave, yet so soft spoken and kind…"

"Ok ok, enough of appreciating her, leave it for when she comes! On a serious note you should get to know her family background. Don't get me wrong but I wouldn't want you to be in trouble."

"Don't worry mom. Everything will be alright. She is really very nice."

Saying this I left from her room and started cleaning my room.

My room looked like that of a five year old. Blue blankets, blue curtains, walls covered with posters of Spiderman, Batman, SpongeBob, and all other cartoons that I was fond of as a kid. In the corner, was a study table which was quit huge. It supported a computer, loads of books, a lamp and a small idol of Lord Ganesha that mom had kept years ago.

Aditi was examining everything around, and said, "When you talk to me you seem a different person, your room tells quite a different story."

"Is it now…"

"You come out as a mature, obedient, studious Aditya but your room is so lively, full of fun and innocence like a kid. And I can't decide which one the real Aditya is!"

"I don't have two sides; it's just that I feel I don't want to let go of the child in me."

"You are really very mysterious, Aditya. A person's room reveals a lot of secrets"

"Oh so what secret did you uncover?"

"Patience, time will reveal all secrets!"

"Ok, let's solve the mystery of chemistry now."

"Sure."

We got so involved in studies that we absolutely lost track of time and we didn't realize that it was 9:30 pm, when mom called us for dinner. Aditi was a little uncomfortable but we still had a lot of ground to cover leaving her with no other option.

"You should call your parents and inform that you are having dinner at our place", I told her.

She thought about it. "No its fine, really."

It was a little weird. I couldn't understand why she felt it was alright. when she was having dinner here and her parents wouldn't even know it. Maybe her parents are out of town or something. I let it be, and continued with dinner.

"How was the dinner Aditi, you liked it?" mom asked her while picking up the plates.

"It was fantastic aunty! The dal was so delicious."

"Thanks dear. Aditya, drop Aditi home if gets too late. I am off to sleep, I have an early start tomorrow. Don't forget to drop her home safely"

"Yes mom, don't worry. Good night"

Aditi and I resumed studies.

Sometime later, Aditi said, "Aditya it's too hot here can we take a break"

"We are about to complete the course, come let's take a break."

"Well don't you have a place in your house that is cooler?"

"Come with me"

I took her upstairs to the terrace.

"Aditya, this is an amazing, open sky, shining stars. We are so close to the sky. There is so much of peace here, no complains, no demands, no anger, only peace… You know, if I ever would want to take a break from my life you will always find me here, somewhere high, above everyone's hate, jealously, fear, just I and this wide sky"

"This world is a lot more than just hate, Aditi. If there is evil, there is good somewhere. Everyone has some goodness in them. It's just that they need a small ray of hope to lighten their dark minds."

"Sometimes a ray of hope is not enough to lighten a room full of despair."

I could feel some pain in her eyes. I decided it was best to change the topic, I had definitely treaded onto difficult terrain here.

"This conversation is getting to heavy. I cannot handle so many philosophic thoughts at once!"

"Oh yes, just pretend you didn't hear any of that, sometimes I really talk crap. What do you feel standing on this terrace?"

"This is my favorite place in my house. Here I feel myself, I feel that life has no bounds, its limitless like this sky, our life should also have no limits we should fly as high as we can. I feel so optimistic when I come to the terrace."

"Oh so now the scholar is being philosophic!"

We both laughed.

"Aditya, can I ask you something?"

"Yes, why not? Shoot!"

"Aditya, you never talk about your father. Is he out somewhere?"

"Yes, he is out, somewhere in this sky, he is one of these stars, shining for mom and me."

"Oh I am so sorry…"

"Don't be. He passed away when I was just four, I don't remember him much. Mom and I have learned to live without him."

"Yes, I know life goes on. Life is like water no matter how tight you hold it in your hands it will slip off."

"You were surprised seeing my room right? Actually my father had designed my room. I don't have many memories with him so I did not want to destroy this one. My room is just as he left it. It makes me feel his presence and consoles me that he is there somewhere seeing me, and being happy when he sees me happy".

"I told you a room tells a lot of secrets"

"Yes, you were right."

We went back downstairs and finished the course. I dropped her home at 11:45, it was almost midnight. No one opened the door for her, she just let herself in. Maybe everyone had gone to bed, so I didn't give it a second thought.

4

Something's cooking?

Our third semester board exams were over. I scored 94% while Aditi scored 91%. Since I scored more, it was my turn to treat her. We didn't want to do a huge party, we settled for a small treat in the school canteen itself. Fortunately, it fit well in my budget.

We met in the canteen. As always, I was five minutes early and she was ten minutes late.

"Well congratulation Aditya! If you perform consistently like this I am sure no one can stop you from getting an admission in IIT... But seriously, thanks a lot for all your help, I would have been able to do none of this without you. Thanks for all your help. And sorry for all the mid-night calls asking numerous doubts and disturbing your sleep"

After she completed her thank you speech, I was so overwhelmed by her words. "I did it just because I know you are friend, I believe you would never leave me alone. And you also helped me a lot in chemistry, so it's the efforts of both of us that we have got such good results."

Lifting up the glass of coke she said," yes your right so cheers to our results"

"Nope! Cheers to our friendship!"

"Oh goodness! How do you manage to say the right thing all the time!"

"Well, that's me!" I said wittily.

We laughed for a while and then drank the Coke. As the exams had ended we decided to take two days break from studies.

With all the time that had gone by, my feelings towards Aditi had become stronger. I had began with thinking it was just an attraction but now it made me realize that this could be true love.

Aditi had accomplished changing my habit of being late at school. Nowadays I always reached school well before time, with a hope to see Aditi again. I would sit on my usual seat and Aditi would come a little late.

"Hi, scholar! How was your break?", she asked one day.

Well, of course it was boring and I was waiting all these days to see her. I did connect with her on Facebook but it wasn't really enough. Our break was just the weekend but it seemed so long like a million years!

"Yeah, it was fine, mostly I got bored…"

"Even mine was a little boring but I am not yet getting the study mood. Two days was so not enough."

"Hey, why not we go for a movie today? I mean if you don't mind?"

The realization dawned upon me a moment later that I was almost broke at the moment and had nearly exhausted my pocket money a couple of days back. I decided to give this treat from my saved pocket money, if she said yes, that is.

"Sure why not! How about Inox multiplex at 7?"

"Fine, I have no problem. Should I pick you up?

Fingers crossed.

"No, no, that won't be necessary. I can come on my own, no need to pick me up."

5

Eyeing Interactions

As always, that day too, I was 5 minutes early and she was 10 minutes late. Having purchased the tickets already, I stood close to the ticket window so I could catch her once she walked in. We were going to watch 'Yeh jawaani hai dewaani', a romcom starring the recent heartthrob Ranbir Kapoor, who happened to be Aditi's favorite actor as well.

And there she walked in, in denim shorts and a casual white top. She wore her hair down and the delicate anklet with a star on her ankle made her look even more beautiful than I already thought her to be.

I was lost in my own thoughts when I heard her ask, "Hey Adi, u got the tickets? And you're looking good today!"

"Thanks, ummm…well you are looking great too. I have the tickets here, so let's go in and take our seats."

"Great! How much are the tickets for?"

"Nope, I am not telling you that, this one's on me"

"Hey Adi, that's not fair! I am going to pay my share. You pay up every time, It's my turn today."

"It's alright. You can pay for the dinner if you want. But the tickets are still on me!"

"When did we decide to go for dinner?", she seemed genuinely shocked.

"Oh, is that a problem? I just thought it would get really late when the movie ends and you must not have had anything to eat since afternoon, so the least I could do is take you for dinner. Its fine if you don't want to."

"No, it's alright, Adi. I would just get very late going home. But it's ok, let's go to our usual café after the movie and that's on me."

A lot of people used to address me as 'Adi', but it felt the best when Aditi did. It sounded sweet when she said it.

All through the movie, I watched her more than I saw the movie. Like it happens in most movies, I kept my hand round her shoulders, and held her hand as a romantic song played in the movie; she didn't seem to object. We even looked into each other's eyes for half a minute! She seemed a little hesitant, and turned away then, staring down at the popcorn in her hand.

We went back to seeing the movie then. I wanted to look into her eyes again, those eyes that conveyed warmth, friendship, attraction and love; all rolled into one amazing casserole. I went back to holding her hand, she didn't quite object, instead she held it tighter. This continued till the end of the movie.

Once the movie was over, we went to the café as planned. Aditi did not bring up anything that had happened during the movie. We talked about random stuff and agreed to start our studies from tomorrow. We kept our meal light, it was almost 11 in the night. After dinner, I insisted her I her home. She resisted like she always did, but agreed later.

We rode on our bike. Much to my chagrin, her house was just a five minute drive from the café. I could feel the cold air on my face, and it felt magically divine, like love is in the air. It was a really special moment for me. I couldn't want life to be more perfect than how it was in this one moment. But life always has other plans for you...

This movie date had turned out to be super awesome. I had never been so happy. I felt it was time to look for the right moment and let Aditi know what I felt for her.

6

Immortal Friendship

The next few days were really hectic. We had lot of tests, assignments and the pressure of exams kept increasing. Yet, the opportunity to spend time with Aditi even made studying fun!

Now my world revolved around only two things – my mom and Aditi. There was a time not so long when school meant books, studies, Krishnanth and boring lectures for me, but now school became so much more fun with Aditi around. We would bunk classes (Aditi's idea, she was the fearless one), trouble teachers, play pranks on Krishnanath and so much more.

One day Mrs. Mitra gave us a physics assignment which Aditi completely forgot about. I had texted her last night about the same but it seems she had ran out her internet pack and hadn't seen the text. I, smitten by Aditi as I was, removed my name from my assignment and wrote hers instead.

Mrs. Mitra shouted out in the class, "Aditi where is your assignment? You know these marks get added to your final results."

Aditi fumbled, "Ma'aam….. I ….have…"

I passed my assignment with her name on it to Aditi and said "Take this, don't worry about me."

She took it over to Mrs. Mitra.

Mrs. Mitra appreciate it. I was up next. "Aditya, where is your assignment?"

"Ma'am sorry I forgot to bring it. I promise I will submit it tomorrow." I tried sounding as convincing as I could.

Mrs. Mitra got terribly angry and said, "Aditya Patel, I did not expect this from you. You are an intelligent, good student. You are always regular. You have disappointed me today. Because you have never missed on any submission ever, I will let you go this time and give you one more day. But, you have to do the assignment twice now."

As it would be, I was saved by the bell announcing end of the class, and Mrs. Mitra left the class. Aditi dragged me out of the class and confronted me, "Why did you do this, what if we had got caught?"

"Aditi, but the fact is, we did not get caught. At least you were saved from her ire. Is Ms. Aditi Sharma scared of Mrs. Mitra? Now that's something!!!" I said with a smile, trying to change the topic.

"No, Aditya I am not afraid of her, I was worried about you. I was ok with her shouting on me or cutting back on my grades, I hadn't done the assignment after all, I wouldn't want you to be in trouble because of me."

"It's fine, Aditi. Nothing really happened..."

This only made her furious, "How will I not worry Aditya!!! I care for you and wouldn't want you to be in trouble."

I was taken aback. "Don't worry Aditi, I wouldn't mind getting into trouble a million times for you."

"Glad to have a friend like you."

The bell rang again. She still thought of me as a friend, and nothing more. Whatever keeps her happy then!

The next class was Chemistry. Shantanu sir, our chemistry teacher, looked no less than Hitler. The few hair he had left, were oiled all the time and he had a big fat mole below his left eye. He always wore a white and yellow checks shirt and brown trousers well above his waist.

For the next hour he kept talking about some boring chemistry concepts and I had no option but to focus on what he was saying, we had a test next week after all.

Aditi and I met in the evening at my place to study chemistry. I baked her favorite chocolate brownie and decided to give her a little surprise. It took a lot of time to prepare it. But I was doing it for Aditi, so it was perfectly alright. When it comes to Aditi, there were two sure shot things to bring a smile on her face –a chocolate brownie or Ranbir kapoor.

She was wearing a deep blue embroidered kurti and dark green leggings. She was really surprised seeing the brownie and her face lit up with joy.

Aditi was one person who would find happiness in the smallest of things. She never expected anything big, but small things mattered a lot to her.

"So why am I getting a gift today?" she said with a big smile.

"Because, I wanted to surprise you today."

"What's the occasion?"

"Well, there is no occasion. It's just a small treat from a friend. Why, can't friends give treats?"

"Of course, they can. They should always keep giving small, sweet and special treats." Saying that, she bit in the brownie.

We went back to our studies then and spent the remainder of the day just studying; we had our Chemistry test the next day. I would steal a glance at her from time to time, couldn't really afford to keep staring and get lost in dreamland.

7

Disappearances

The next day after getting done with our chemistry test we decided to take a break from studies. It was Aditi who decided actually. She wanted to take a break from studies for a day or two. The next subject in the study queue was Mathematics and Aditi was never really bored with it but she decided not to meet in the evening.

She seemed casual when she said it, but her eyes betrayed her words. There was definitely something going on in her head. I didn't want to pry too much and decided not to ask. I was unsure if I had seen fear in her eyes. This was unlike anything I had seen before, not even remotely like the Physics-phobia she had.

"Hey Aditi, are you alright?" I was genuinely concerned.

"Absolutely! What could happen to me?"

I did not take it any further and decided to give her some space.

The next day I went to school hoping maybe Aditi would share what was bothering her. To my utter dismay, she remained absent the entire day in school. I was getting restless, I hadn't talked to her in an entire day! I wanted to know if she was alright. I was totally unable to focus on anything that went on in the class. I just could not stop thinking about her. I kept telling myself I was over-reacting, but that didn't calm me down either. I rushed out of the class, as soon as the bell announced the break. I went to the parking lot, took out my phone (of course cell phones are not allowed in the school premises). My call went unanswered. I tried twice, thrice but there was no reply. Disheartened and even more worried now, I went back to class. She did not show up in class the next day either. It only bothered me more

Both the days in the evening, I waited outside our usual café, hoping to see her, but she did not show up. I would go back home and open my books to study. But I could not pretend any more, I could not concentrate on anything. I kept thinking that something must be wrong, Aditi just wouldn't miss school for two consecutive days, as attendance mattered a lot in our school, especially in the 12th grade.

Next morning, I reached school half an hour before. I wanted to catch hold of her as soon as she came in. Everyone came, the classes started but there was no sign of her. I pretended to be sick and went back home in the lunch break itself. By then, I had 92 missed calls and 102 messages to Aditi by that time. I just couldn't reach her.

The next day without giving it the slightest thought of how her family would react, I went to her house. Her Scooty was not there. I rang the bell but there was no one in the house. I peeped through the window. The house seemed uncleaned. Everything was covered with a layer of dust and there were spider webs all around. It didn't seem like anyone had lived in this house in years.

I asked about Aditi to Mr. Desai, the neighbor. I was told she had gone to the school. I was relieved. I immediately started my bike and drove as fast as I could. I saw her Scooty parked in her regular place and rushed to the class to see her. But to my despair, she was not in the class. I did not know where to go, where would she be? I calmed down. I closed my eyes, and thought of her. I thought that in these days I must know something about her. I remembered the night we went to the terrace. She said whenever she wanted to take a break I will find her above everyone's hate.

8

Moment of Revelation

It hit me then and I ran to the school terrace as fast as I could. This was my last hope. And, there she was, sitting in a corner, her arms around her knees and head bent down. I went up to her and sat down next to her. I had never seen her like this. I was happy to find her but she seemed sad. I could not bear to see her like this.

"Aditi what happened? I called you and texted you so many times, but there was no reply, I was worried about you."

This only made her furious, she stood up and began shouting, "Why Aditya, why did you call me? Why did you text me? Why are you so concerned about me? I know at the end of the day you are also going to leave me, like everyone. Nobody wants me in their life."

"Aditi calm down, why would I do that? Why would anybody want to do that?"

"Liar! All of this that you are doing, is fake. I know that."

"No Aditi, it's not like that. Calm down."

She got angrier and got even louder, "You know nothing, Aditya. If there was any good left in this world my own aunt would not have done this to me..."

"Aditi, Calm down. Tell me what happened. I am right here for you, I will always be there for you."

She took a long, deep breath and calmed down.

"I don't know what to tell you Aditya. I feel so jealous when I see you and your mom. She cares so much for you, she loves you so much. I don't have anyone like that, nobody loves me. I just bring bad luck to everyone."

"No Aditi, there are always people who love you, you just have to look around. You are not any bad luck."

"My mother died because of me, you want to still say that to me?"

I was taken aback for a moment, I didn't know what to say. She broke down into tears. She continued, "My mother was the daughter of the owner of a big IT company. My father was working there as a Sr. engineer. They met and fell for each other. My mother was just 17 then. My dad was much older. Mom got pregnant. The day when she was going to tell him, he vanished, just disappeared into thin air. She had gone to the office to meet him, but his desk was cleared. She got to know that he had resigned long ago as he had got a better job in America. No call, no message, no letter, nothing. He had left behind nothing. My mom was shattered. My mom tried a lot to reach him. He even picked her call one day and do you know what he said? He said, "I don't care about your baby. I have come too far now, just get the hell out of my life. If you want to abort the baby you can it's your choice but now I am not going to turn back. I don't want to destroy my career at this point of time." Due to the teenage pregnancy mom had a lot of complications, she was under a lot of stress. She died giving birth to me. My grandfather brought me up then. He told me everything when I turned 13. He passed away that year. Then I went to stay with my maternal uncle and aunt. But they never treated me like family, I was always an outsider. My aunt would torture me saying I was unlucky for the family. Wherever I would go I would bring bad luck, that I was good for nothing. I would never have wanted any of this to happen, it wasn't my fault. I was a burden for my uncle and aunt. During summer vacations my uncle, my aunt and my cousins would go out, but never took me along. I would alone at home. I felt so helpless. I was dependent on them. But now I am not. Whenever you would come to drop me home I deliberately took you to my old house where my grandfather and I lived, I did not want my aunt to see us. Since the day we went to see the movie, whenever I would reach home late she would make it a big problem. She didn't care for me or worry about me. She just got another chance to tell me I was a spoiled, irresponsible person like my father. After the chemistry test, when I went home and she was taunting me as she always did. I couldn't take it anymore. So, I told her that it was just enough and I couldn't take it anymore. With that, she threw me out of the house, on the road, all alone. To be alone is written in my fate. So, don't try becoming a part of my life Aditya, you will also throw me out of your life, like everyone else has. You will.."

I didn't let her complete the sentence. "Sssshhh, not a word more. Your turn to listen now."

I took her hand in mind and told her, Today, I make a promise to you that I not leave you, not so easily anyways. I will always be there with you, for you. And this is not fake. I mean every word I said. Aditi, I love you and I mean it"

"We make promises to break them, Aditya..."

As she said this, a tear rolled down from her eyes. I wiped it off and said, "The day I will lose you that day I will lose myself. I will not be your shadow which vanishes in dark, I will be the ray of hope in your life. Trust me here, I really love you Aditi, I can't imagine a life without you."

She hugged me as tight as she could. I hugged her back. My life felt complete in that one moment.

"I love you too Aditya, I love you too. I won't leave you either, you will have to tolerate me your whole life.."

She started to feel a little better.

"Well, I would love to tolerate for all eternity!"

We remained still for a moment. I wish time could have stopped in that one moment.

Just then, it hit us that we were still in school and we had missed the entire morning session of classes. We decided to quietly get back to our class before we get caught. But we were out of luck, and Shantanu sir caught us sneaking in. He took us to the Principal's office. We made up a story that Aditi was sick, and so she had to be taken to the hospital. So, we were asked to produce a medical certificate. We didn't know what to do but we were allowed to sit in the class. We had until tomorrow to produce the certificate.

"Are you alright?", I asked Aditi.

"Yeah Adi, I was just thinking about the certificate. I don't want you to be in trouble because of me."

"Don't worry, I will find a way out. Take care, and call me if you need anything. Let's meet in the evening and study together."

"No, Adi you don't have to miss your studies for me. I can manage myself."

"But Aditi you have a lot to manage already. I went by your old house this morning, it's just in a livable state. It would take way too long to do it alone. Let me help and then we can study together."

"No Adi, its fine..."

"Fine, whatever the lady wishes. You set up your house I will try and get a medical certificate."

When I went home I just realized that I had got something that I wanted since a long time. Aditi whom I loved so much, loved me too. Was it a dream? I so happy! I danced with mom when I saw her. She asked why I was so happy, I couldn't hold it anymore and I told her everything.

That was a mistake. I should have taken some time to digest everything before I could tell anybody else.

"Adi, I told you to be careful, her own relatives are not accepting her so there must be some reason behind it. You are in Class XII, you have your own ambitions. You can't afford to get distracted. It was fine till you were friends. You're just 17, you have a whole life ahead of you. It isn't an age to decide and think about love"

"Mom, what happened with Aditi was not at all her fault. And mom, love knows no limits, it knows no age. Do we ever decide and fall in love? It is a beautiful feeling that just happens."

"Aditya, I am your mom, and I know what love is. But life has its own rules. It's unpredictable. The most beautiful things give the most pain. I don't want you to suffer the pain the way I did. It's not that I am asking you never to fall or believe in love, it's just that I don't think this is the right time. And I don't think Aditi is appropriate either."

"Don't worry Mom. Everything will be alright. Trust me. I won't let any of this come in the way of my dreams."

"Well then, it's your life, do as you please. I am there to support you to the best I can."

"Mom, you are the best mom ever!"

9

The story begins

With the Class XII Board exams fast approaching, all of my cousins – three sisters and four brothers, dropped by to wish me luck. There was still few days to go, however, they did not want to disturb me later. And as cousins go, we are always on the lookout for a reason to meet and have a blast.

We are one family, but we are miles apart from each other. My cousins, Sumit and Sanket, are twins, and the only thing common between the two is their age. My brother Ronit is a year younger to me while Aarav is a year older to me. Aarav is the studious one. My sister Ayesha is in school, Nandini di and Natasha di are elder to me. Natasha is pursuing her degree in Physiotherapy while Nandini has completed her degree from med school and is currently completing her internship.

Of all my cousins, I have been closest to Nandini di, as I lovingly call her, she has always been my secret keeper. Studies have kept me busy and it's been a while since I met her. As we often did, we had gathered at my place, and checking out each other's phones. I was lost in my world, as had often become the case lately. I was occupied in my text conversation with Aditi.

"Busy?" I wanted to check if she was busy, I didn't intend to disturb her.

55 seconds later I had my response, "How can I study, my prince charming is not letting me concentrate. You know my new hobby is day dreaming. As soon as I open my book he comes in my dreams. He is bothering me from a long time. :P :P"

I couldn't help smile. I wasn't surprised when Nandini di noticed.

"Oh so he is bothering you, right? Maybe I should ask him to find another princess then :P :P"

"No one can steal him from me. Ask him if you please. He will never agree to go to any other princess. He won't leave me."

"So much trust in him!!! And what if he breaks your heart? :P :P"

"Don't you dare talk anything like this about him. He is just made for me. And I trust him more than myself. And I know he loves me more than anyone on this earth! :* :*"

"But what's the use if the Princess does not love him back! :P"

"Who said the princess does not love him. Her love is much more than that of the Prince."

"Well love cannot be measured. It's eternal and boundless. Well, now the prince needs some rest. Bye, take care. :* :*"

"Bye <3"

I had to cut the conversation short as everyone had gathered around me. If anybody caught a glimpse of the messages I would be in a lot of trouble. They would never stop teasing me about it and pulling my leg.

But Nandini di had noticed everything and had understood. She had seen how my face lit up whenever Aditi's message came.

Rony and Aarav were sitting on my study table. Rony was busy with his mobile phone, may be texting his 50th girlfriend and Aarav picking his brains trying to figure out who Rony was actually texting. Sumit, Sanket and Natasha were as usual pulling Ayesha's leg sitting on the bed, she was the youngest amongst us.

I was sitting at one corner of the bed. Nandini di quietly came sat next to me. She asked me playfully, "So what's cooking little brother?"

"Nothing! Nothing is cooking!"

"Oh, please! I know you since you used to wear superman costumes and roam around in the whole house. I have never seen you blushing like this. And the Aditya I know is never so busy staring at his phone, smiling and typing away…You never used to know where you had kept your phone at all!! Show me whom were you texting…"

She snatched my phone from me but couldn't see any messages; it had a lock screen, of course!

She turned to me and said, "Seriously!!! This is breaking news! I think I should tell everyone."

"No, no di please, don't tell anyone, please, they will kill me. They are not going to spare me", I pleaded.

"Then tell me what's going on"

"Ok, Ok I'll tell you the whole story. But please can we go somewhere else, I don't want anyone to overhear us."

"Ok let's go out in the living room."

"Not like this. Give me a minute", I said softly. I said out aloud then, "Di, mom was asking if you could help make arrangements for lunch"

"Sure! I should go, you should also come and help."

As I was following Nandini Di out of my room, I heard Roney saying, "How will Aditya help in making arrangements for lunch?"

On this Natasha di said, "I don't know why they sometimes act so weird"

I did not react as there was a point in Roney's question. Ignoring everything I went out in the verandah. We both sat on the swing. I told Nandini Di everything, from the start.

"Fascinating love story Aditya. I had never thought that you would fall for a girl so easily."

"You know Di, if it's not written in our destiny a whole life time is not enough to realize true love. But if it's written, only one moment is enough to fall in love."

"OMG! Now I can see, you have changed a lot."

"Some people, they just enter your life and in a second everything totally changes in you, around you, everywhere, like it was a beautiful miracle you never thought would happen"

"Maybe this miracle is really love then…"

"Well this miracle is Aditi…"

My phone buzzed just then, Aditi had sent me a text. She was asking about the medical certificate.

"Oh no! I seriously forgot about this."

Di asked me if there was a problem.

"Yup, di. I told you about the morning on the terrace. Aditi and I had missed the entire morning session. When we were on our way back to class, the teacher caught us and took us to the Principal. We made up a story that Aditi was not well and had to be taken to the hospital. So we were asked to produce a medical certificate. I completely forgot about it, and now I don't know what to do"

"Stop grumbling, this is nothing. You forgot I am a doctor now, I could help you if you want me to…"

"Goodness! How could I forget this? Really Di you are a Godsend! Should I say Dr. Nandini?"

We laughed at that, and Nandini di would write out the medical certificate to cover for our story.

We had our lunch and it was time for the cousins to leave.

"Thanks a lot, Di I feel much better after talking to you now."

"You don't need to thank me, we are family, right?"

"Yes, Di we are all for one and one for all!"

10

On cloud nine

After the lunch that day, I kept everything else in my head aside and focused on my studies. Aditi would kill me if I hadn't done that and ended up at her place. At around 2PM, I decided to study stay focused on the books for at least another 4-5 hours, however, by the time it was 5, I was began getting really restless and getting distracted thinking about Aditi, and tried my best to focus on the task at hand. It was only getting more and more difficult now. I stretched on till 6:15PM and that was it, I couldn't hold up anymore.

With that, I changed into my jeans and T-shirt and was on my way out in less than five minutes. Just as I was starting my bike, I called out to mom, "Mom I am going to Aditi's place. We are going to study together and I will also help her setup her house. I might get late there, so will let you know if I would be able to make it for dinner."

"Call me as soon as you can. I am just about starting to fix the dinner. And don't be too late."

"Yes Mom, bye!"

With that, I sped off, driving as fast as I could. If ever mom found out the speed at which I was driving, I was sure to get grounded.

I reached her place and rang the doorbell. Aditi must have been busy in something; she took a lot of time to answer the bell. She opened the door but her attention was somewhere else, she kept dusting her clothes. She had cleaned up the house, and now she needed to clean up herself, she was covered with dust from head-to-toe.

"Ahem, ahem", I coughed a little to grab attention.

She looked up; her eyes told she was happy seeing me. She opened her arms to hug me but stopped as she remembered the layers of dust she had accumulated on herself with the entire day spent in cleaning. I stepped forward anyways, hugged her tight and said softly, "You are beautiful and pure from inside, I don't really care about anything else, and whatever happens you will always be here, in my arms".

She smiled and blushed. She looked up for a moment and pulled me back into her arms. "Let's just stay like this forever and ever. We could remain as we are for the whole life time and agree to accept and respect each other, no matter what", she said in a very soft voice.

After a moment we realized that we were outside her house and passers-by could see us. We separated as if nothing had happened, and I asked her playfully, "You haven't yet asked me to come inside, do you want to keep something for once we are inside?"

She laughed and it just made me love her even more when she did so. "I don't really have a problem if that's what you wish, after all, jab pyar kiya toh darna kya!", I said throwing in a very filmy dialogue.

"Shut up Adi, all the neighbors can see us, stop it!"

"Ok, but let me come in at least."

"Yeah sure."

She closed the door from inside.

"Your intentions don't seem very good here…" I laughed as I teased her.

"Shut up now Adi, I have a lot of work to do."

"Fine, Ms.Busy. This Princess has no time for her Prince. He should go and find someone else."

I went towards the door and acted as if I was going to leave. Aditi stopped me and pushed me towards the wall, "Adi please, I am really stressed right now. Don't you get it? We have not got the medical certificate, the principal will kill us tomorrow. And top of it this house seems a haunted place and I haven't studied a single word in a long, long time. Nothing looks fine."

I kept my finger on her lips to quiet her. "Ssshhh, you grumble a lot. We both are together right now. What can be more proper than this?"

I took out the medical certificate from my pocket. "What is this?"

"This is a doctor's prescription!"

"Adi!" she retorted angrily.

"Obviously Aditi, it's your medical certificate, what did you think?"

"Wow, Adi you did it, you are seriously Godsend. I am so happy and relieved."

She hugged me tight as she said that. She looked up and came closer to me, as if she wanted to kiss me. However, I moved away and did not let it happen. I thought that we should take it a little slow. I was feeling overwhelmed from being so happy and I feared I might lose it. I used to believe that happiness is accompanied by some or the other sadness, neither of them ever struck alone. But this time, I refused to go with my beliefs and did not want any sadness to befall us.

"But how did you get it?" she seemed confused.

"Well it's a long story I will tell you some other day. Right now we have a lot of work to do."

I helped Aditi with the remaining cleaning - removing the cobwebs, wiping furniture clean to bring it back to a usable state; and making the house livable overall. It took some time. As we washed our hands clean after finishing up with the cleaning, I splashed some water on Aditi.

"Adi, you must not be doing this! You want to play; really, I will show you how to play."

A mug full of water was kept on the platform beside. It got emptied in a moment on me.

"Now you must not be doing this! Now you are going to pay for this!"

I ran behind her taking a bottle of water. She stood up on the couch. "Aditi come down yar, this is cheating. Then don't blame me for spoiling your couch."

"Well the bottle is with you; you are the one spilling the water, so the blame is on you."

"Ok, now how will you escape this one?"

I pulled her down towards me, off the couch. Doing that, I lost balance me and slipped backwards on the floor. The bottle in my hand fell on the ground and the water spilled on the floor. She fell over me. For a moment she was lying on me. I could not take my eyes off her. We were still like that for a while. I left her hands which I had held as I had pulled her towards me. She came closer to hug me but suddenly something came to her mind and she got up. I also tried to get up but was unable to. I had not realized that I had injured the back of my head a bit as I had fallen backwards.

"Adi are you alright? Do you need something?" she sounded worried.

"Yes, I am totally fine and I don't need anything."

Now the floor we had just cleaned had water spilt all over it. I was about to tell Aditi that I won't clean it, when she said, "Don't worry I will clean it."

We cooked pasta for dinner. I helped with cutting vegetables and serving. She did everything else, and I was just cracking jokes and having fun.

"Do you know Aditya Patel you are getting lazier day by day." She said adding the final ingredients to the pasta.

"Oh yes, and now you have come in my life so now it's your responsibility to make me more and more lazy."

"As His Majesty orders, I better do it or else this Prince will find some other Princess and that I cannot afford."

"Now that's like a good girl."

I pulled her closer and said, "Don't you worry this Prince is not going to leave you so early!"

"Well in that case, the Prince has to prove it."

"And how do you want him to prove it?"

"How about by serving dinner tonight?"

"Yes, that I can definitely do. Your Highness can take a seat now this kitchen is under full control of the Great Prince Aditya Patel!"

As we were having out dinner and I had a thought. I asked her, "Aditi if you promise not to get angry, could I ask you something?"

"Yes, of course Adi, you can ask whatever you like."

"Aditi I don't want to bring up or discuss anything about your past, I know it is painful for you. But where were you those three days that you remained absent in school? I have been wondering and wondering about that. You weren't at home, you weren't in school; so where were you?"

She did not speak for a while, I thought I might have chartered some forbidden painful territory and decided to back off, "It's alright if you don't want to talk about it, it's perfectly fine. You can take your time. I know I should give you your space. And you really don't have to answer all question. Whenver you want to talk about anything, I will be right here; there is nothing you need to worry about. You just have to ask, and no matter where I will be, I will run to be at your side"

"Yes, Aditya I know that. There is no one else in my life, except you, you will be the first person I call if anything happens. When my aunt threw me out of the house I didn't know what to do, I was totally blank. I thought if I remain in the same city I will never forget what happened and will not be able to move on. So I decided to go in an entirely new city. I bought a ticket to Ahmedabad from the money I had saved. I felt that maybe unknown streets and unknown people would help me to forget old stories. But it worsened me. I went there but my mind was still here. There I had to start from finding a place to live, school and everything, here at least I had my scholarship at the school and my grandfather's house. So I changed my mind and came back. Meanwhile, I also saw your messages and realized that there was someone who cared for me and is concerned about me. And I came back."

"I am glad you realized it soon, I couldn't imagine being so far from you."

After dinner, we went to the terrace and sat down. I lied down with my head in her lap.

"Long day, huh?" I said in a sleepy tone.

"Yes indeed"

"And you still look so fresh and energetic. Don't you ever get tired Aditi?"

"Well what good is it if young people like you and me get tired so easily? If life does not get tired of challenging us then why should we get tired challenging it!"

"You have a point."

I got up and pulled her to stand up as well.

"What are you doing Aditya?"

"You just said that we should never get tired. We should remain energetic, so don't you think rather than sitting and chit chatting here like old people we should celebrate our special day."

"Hmmmm"

"Hmmmm"

I played the songs on my cell phone. I pulled her close and we danced on some romantic songs. We both were lost in each other eyes. I pulled her closer and we hugged each other tight. She clung on to me long after. After a while she left me and kissed me on my forehead. She blushed and turned her back towards me. We knew our limits and this was where we drew the line.

I quickly changed the song and kept a party number, pulling up the volume rocker to full blast. We danced like crazy. I could not remember when would be the last time I had danced so freely.

"Ok, Aditya we have had enough for today. Leave some craziness for tomorrow."

"Yes, it's quiet late." I had 18 missed calls from mom, the phone was on complete silent mode.

"Oh crap, I had totally forgotten about this!"

"What happened?"

"I was supposed to call mom and inform her if I would be coming home for dinner. She told me to reach home in time. Its 1:25am, I am in so much trouble today."

"Aditya how could you be so irresponsible. Aunty must be worried. Now run fast, and reach safely. Don't forget to text me once you reach. I will be awake till then."

"Yes, I will."

11

Possessive, Protective, Mom

All along the ride back home, my mind was occupied with a million thoughts. That one moment in which I fell in love with Aditi had changed me so much. If just one moment could change so much, one day could do so much more. But the day was not over yet. I had to go home and face mom. I was worried about how angry she would be and how she would vent out her anger. I silently opened the door and tiptoed inside. I hoped mom would have gone to bed by now and very quietly peeped in her room. Far from asleep, she was reading her favorite Sudha Murthy novel the 100th time!!!

"Come in Adi, I know you are at the door."

Moms tend to have this strange sixth sense with which they seem to know just everything about you.

"Mom, I am really very sorry. I should have called you but it just slipped out from my mind…"

She did not let me complete my explanation. She began shouting, "Adi, it's almost 1:45 in the night. How could you have become so irresponsible? I have been waiting for you since when! I kept thinking that maybe you were busy but you will call me in a while, but there is not even a single message from you! You know how worried I have been? You were never like this before, you have never kept your Mom alone like this. You forgot me just because of that girl whom you have known since only a few months? This is what I struggled and sacrificed so much for?"

"No, Mom it's not because of her. It's not her fault."

"Then tell me why did you not call me? Why did you not return any of my calls? Why did you not answer any of my calls? Why did you not even to inform me if you would come home for dinner?"

"Mom you are over reacting now. What's such a big deal if I did not call you once. Why are you shouting so much? I did not commit any crime."

"So now I am overreacting? Seriously? Adi, I have not eaten anything since afternoon just because I was waiting for you."

"So who told you to remain hungry? I didn't ask you to wait up for me and stay hungry! If you are hungry, you should have eaten!" With that, I crossed the line and raised my voice really high.

"Aditya is this the way you talk to your mother? Is this what I taught you?" Mom shouted on the top of her voice.

I realized my folly, I had been really rude and harsh, I should not have done that, but how could I take her holding Aditi responsible for me not coming home for dinner. It took me a while to calm down.

I went to the kitchen and took some rajma-chawal that Mom had prepared for dinner in a plate and went to mom's room. She was still reading the novel. I took the novel from her hand and kept it down.

"Mom I am really very sorry. I don't know what happened to me. I should not have talked to you like I did. I understand you were worried about and I am sorry for not calling you. I know you are my greatest well-wisher and you cannot see any harm come to me. I am really sorry, please say something now!"

She remained quiet. I could realize she was deeply hurt. Up until now she had always been my first priority, but now she was sharing this place with Aditi. So I guess problems were bound to occur.

"Mom don't you always say that it's important that someone realize their mistake, we should forgive them or else they have to regret it their whole life. I have realized my mistake mom, please forgive me."

"Ok, ok, enough, enough of this melodrama. So what have you learned from this whole incident?"

"I realized that mom, you will always be the first priority in my life…"

"No Adi, you are mistaken again. I know I can understand that as life progresses our priorities change. I just want you to never forget me like this. I mean how could you forget that your Mom was waiting for you for dinner."

"Mom today I seriously got carried away and I am sorry."

"Yes, that's exactly my point. I don't want you to get carried away like this. I know love makes you strong but it has its own world. Once you enter this world I don't want you to forget everything else. Today you have forgotten me, some other day you will forget your dreams, and who knows you will just disappear one day, what will I do then? Where will I go? I don't have anyone else besides you…" Mom was almost on the verge of tears.

"Mom don't worry I am not going anywhere. Just the way you need me, I need you too. At the end of the day I will always be in need your lap to lie down and relax and forget all that's bothering me." I fed her some rajma chaval as I said that.

"The rajma hasn't turned out too well today, maybe because I was worried and upset. Good you ate dinner at Aditi's place!"

We both laughed and I slept in her room that night.

So now I had two women in my life who depended and counted on me. I had no idea how I would strike a balance between the two. We generally tended to take the ones we care for, for granted. But this wasn't a mistake I could afford to make either with mom again or with Aditi. I did not want to sacrifice either Mom or Aditi or my dreams. I realized it was going to be difficult but then what in life comes easy? I made up my mind that I would give equal priority to both.

But… Don't they say, man proposes and God disposes?

12

Dreams wake to reality

From the next day, Aditi and I were back to focusing on our studies. With Aditi living by herself in her grandfather's house, our study place shifted from my place to hers. There was nobody to disturb us at her place and mom would also not be around, so she wouldn't get annoyed and worry that I was giving up on my dreams by being with Aditi. Thanks to Aditi, our studies had become so much fun. We would use associate silly things with chemistry to remember concepts and fundamentals.

With the exams fast approaching, school would get over by 12:30 in the afternoon every day, after which I would quickly rush home, grab a quick lunch and reach Aditi's place by 1:30. We would study sincerely till 6:30 in the evening and then take time out to be spend together.

"You are late Mr.!" she said as she opened the door one day.

"Well don't you want to know the reason why am I late today?"

"I just know you are late, so you should be given a punishment. You could give me any reason to be late!"

"Ok, your highness. Whatever you order"

I went near her to kiss her. She avoided it and said, "Enough can you do the remaining romance inside please. One day these neighbors are going to throw me out of the house."

"Aree, how dare they throw you out of your house? I mean can they throw great, courageous "The Aditi Sharma" out of her own house? Don't they know that if they drive you out of your house, you will also not let them live in theirs! One furious look from you and the living daylights would get scared out of them!"

With that Aditi gave her furious look to me. Wide eyes, anger all over her face…

"Yes, I was talking about this one. But don't have to give it to me; you have to give it to them…"

"Don't forget, if this look can scare them, it could also be used to scare you!" She smiled a tiny little bit as she said that.

"Hold on, hold on to this expression. I can get scared of your furious look, but your problem is that you just cannot resist smiling when you see me. And then this smile does not scare me anymore. It makes me fall in love with you all over again."

She blushed and did not say a word.

"And well, you do look a lot more beautiful when you are silent!"

"Adi!!!!" she said hitting me lovingly. I held her hand and brought her close. She hugged me tight.

"See you made me forget why I was late today. Mom was preparing cake for Sumit and Sanket as it is their birthday today. They are my twin brothers I had told you about, remember?"

"Yes, I remember. But then don't you have to go to their party?" "No, actually they came home, I wished them there itself. Being in Class XII and get you an exemption from all parties and occasions."

"Well, that's nice."

"I was waiting for Mom to finish the cake, so I could bring a little for you!"

"Oh, it was fine. I just had lunch."

"Why did you wait for me for such a long time?" I said talking to the cake, "Mom made you with so much of care and affection, and I brought you especially for this lovely lady here and she has no value of it. But don't you worry, I care for you, o sweet one. I will eat you up!"

"Ok, ok enough of the cake-talk. I will eat the cake, but I have a condition."

"Ahan, go ahead."

"You will have to feed me, I will not eat it myself."

"Of course, why not. More than happy to be of service!!!" I said feeding her a piece of the cake.

We started studying in Aditi's room, sitting on her bed. A huge pile of books was there by my side and all the pens and other necessary stationery was next to her. She mentioned she hadn't fully understood one of the Physics numerical we had been solving and so I helping her understand it, while she went through the fundamentals that went behind the numerical.

She wanted one of the reference books that sat next to me while my pen chose the same moment to stop working so I needed another one. We both stretched over the other side to take what we needed and dashed into each other. For a moment we forgot we were in the middle of solving a Physics question and it was study time. As we often did these days, we began looking into each other's eyes and relished the moment.

She came close to me and I thought maybe she was going to kiss me, but she just whispered, "Don't get distracted, patience, after 6:30 it's just us!"

We went back to our books and questions and numerical. I gave her the book she was looking for and she gave me the pen. She had tried to convince me to focus on the studies, but my mind and my eyes would keep wandering over to her. Without looking up from her book she said, "Adi, there's 1 more hour to go. So stop staring before I get annoyed!"

"Time's up! Can we take a break now, please?" It was 6:25 in the evening. Aditi, being the perfectionist that she is, said,

"Adi, there are still 5 minutes left. Can't you wait for just five more minutes?"

"Aditi I am bored to death now. We have been studying since 1:30 in the afternoon."

"To be accurate, Mr. Aditya you came late today."

By that time it was already 6:30.

"See you wasted these five minutes arguing. Instead we could have relaxed and rewound for five more minutes!"

"No, no, no, no…I didn't, you wasted five minutes. We could have studied for five more minutes."

"Oh, is it? Should I take a minute to remind you that you always come everywhere ten minutes late and I always reach everywhere five minutes early?"

"Ok, fine! You win! Now do you want to waste the next whole hour arguing? I definitely wouldn't mind!"

"Of course not! I have no intentions of wasting one precious hour I could spend with you, arguing. Let's go out and sit in the living room. I am bored sitting in one place and seeing the same wall every time I look up."

We went out in the living room. I sat on the floor with my back leaning onto the couch. Aditi went to bring Coke from the fridge.

Vadodara, if you have ever been here then you would know, is always scorching hot. A cold drink could give some respite from the heat.

"Why are you sitting down on the ground?" she asked settling next to me.

"Well, because I am very down to earth, you know…"

"Shut up Adi, that was a really lame one!"

She rested her head on my shoulder, I kept my hand around her.

"So what's going on in your mind?" she asked me.

"Nothing…"

"You are a pathetic liar, Adi!"

"Well I was thinking how the day we get married would be the best day of our life. The whole hall would be filled with lots and lots of nicely dressed people. My mom would be more nervous than me doing the preparations. You would walk down in a gorgeous red lehenga…"

She interjected and said, "Well, I don't like red."

"So make it pink you will look beautiful in any color! So where was I? You enter in a pink lehenga, and you are would be the most beautiful bride one could have ever seen. It would be the happiest day of my life.."

"It would be the happiest day of my life too, but I have a different picture of it. I am sorry, but I don't share you're here."

"Go on"

"I think that, and don't take me wrong for this, but if by taking seven rounds around the holy fire, two people could be tied together by the sacred ties of matrimony, then no marriage would have disintegrated or led to divorces and separations ever, there would only be 'happily ever after's. But that's not how it is, is it? I feel it's only the love and faith between two people that keeps them together, not the rituals. People separate when the love fails to keep them together anymore. When that happens, marriage holds no meaning anymore. I believe, all these customs and traditions are myths created by people. God never came and told us to do so, did He? Then why waste time, energy and money, when you can just sign a paper and get it done with."

"You've got a point there, but families don't necessarily buy that point.."

The mention of families saddened her. I tried to cheer her up and promised, "Don't worry; I'll take you somewhere far, far away. We will leave everyone behind and create a new world for ourselves."

13

Time flies

I reached home at 11:30 that night, but this time I had called mom in the evening to inform her that I would be late and I wouldn't be having dinner with her. Mom was still angry with me. She felt that if I had so much time to spend with Aditi, then I could as well make it to Sumit and Sanket's birthday party. I was getting wary of all those arguments. I didn't know to make mom see the fact that Aditi and I met to study, not to have fun. I still decided to give it a shot one last time. "Mom please believe me, we just study there, we do not waste our time on anything else."

"Adi, you studied even before she came in your life. You have cleared exams earlier and passed with flying colors. You didn't need her then the way you need her now. I am ok with you hanging out with her, but I don't like you being so dependent on her. Your life was going well even without her." she shouted on me.

"But mom now she is a part of my life. I know I can pass this exam without her. But there will be no meaning in it. I will not be satisfied, I will keep feeling incomplete. She completes me in a way nobody else has. If I pass the exams without her, I would feel no joy in it." My voice got louder now, I could not take it anymore.

"Fine, do what you want, just stop picking fights with me because of her."

Well, wasn't it mom who was refusing to understand and kept on arguing. All my life, I have known quite a few women - Nandini Di, mom, Aditi and everyone had one thing in common – overreacting. Women overreact on everything at the drop of a hat. I told myself that the matter would be put to rest once I am done with the exams. Meanwhile I decided to continue focusing on my studies, as if I didn't already do it!!!

A lot of things had happened this semester, time had literally flown. It had been four months since Aditi and I had embarked on a relationship together. Wasn't it just yesterday that I had laid my heart out to her? I could still feel the soft wind on the terrace at my place on that lovely night as I stood there and counted the stars with Aditi. I could feel Aditi's pain as she cried on the school terrace. And in the four months since then, Aditi hasn't cried, I was always there for her. It felt like a huge achievement. With each passing day, Aditi was getting more and more worried about the exams.

"Adi, I really need to score good grades to secure an admission in a government college. I cannot afford a private one. I know my grandfather has left behind a small fortune for me and I have been using it for my survival however, I have my future ahead of me, and I need to think about that as well."

"You don't need to worry so much. We have worked really hard and I am sure it won't go vain. And then I am always there for you, no matter what. Just stay calm and strong. And no one can stop you from achieving what you want."

Finally the countdown had started. The Board exams were set to begin on 8 March that year. Aditi and I decided not to meet beginning 28 Feb and meet only after our exams ended on 14 March. Undoubtedly, mom was the happiest when she heard about this. The next fortnight was to be the most difficult and the longest fortnight of our lives.

On 7 March, not able to contain ourselves, we decided to do a video chat, but for only 10 minutes. We were really desperate to see each other. So, there we were, dialing into our Skype. For a moment, we both didn't know what to say. We just kept looking at each other.

I decided to break the silence, "Why are you staring at me as if you are seeing me for the first time?"

"Well whenever I see you, I fall in love with you all over again, and I am enjoying this feeling after a long time."

"Oho, someone is in a romantic mood today! Ms. Aditi Sharma, I hope you remember that tomorrow is our final Physics board examination?"

"Adi please, don't spoil the mood. The last thing I want to be reminded of right now, are the exams. Why should I worry? I have my lucky charm with me!"

"Great! So, if I am your lucky charm, who will be the one for me?"

"Your mom could be your lucky charm. She will always be with you."

I was at a loss of words. There was such a world of difference between what mom thought about Aditi and how Aditi thought about mom. Aditi respected my mom so much.

"Yes, you are right on this. But all this love for mom! Nothing for me!"

"Yes, because there would be no you without her. And what would I do without you? I might have died long ago, had you not been there for me"

"Oh Aditi, don't talk about dying, we both are going to live together a hundred years. And with that, time's up. Will meet soon. Love you. Bye."

"Love you too. Bye."

14

Showtime

The first exam was physics, then math and then chemistry. We had a day off between the math and chemistry exams, and we had another day off after the chemistry exam. Then we had our English language studies exam, followed by the final exam – Computer Sciences. Except math, all the exams seemed pretty easy.

Since the past 10 years, this year's math exam was said to be the toughest. I had worked really very hard with Aditi and didn't think it should pose a problem. I expected a good score 85% in it. However, Aditi's exam didn't go well, she was really disappointed.

I tried my best to cheer her up, we still had three more exams to go. It wasn't a time to break down over bygones. This was a time to forget what had happened and focus on the upcoming exams.

The entire time that stayed away from each other due to the exams, we would talk twice a day, once after the exam was done, and once before going to bed. Aditi believed she would be unable to fall asleep if she didn't talk to me before going to bed. That made it my duty to call her each night, while it was hers to call me after the exam.

The only time this didn't happen was after the Math exam, I naturally assumed that she must have been really disappointed with how she had fared at the exam. I decided to call her, "Hi! Your lucky charm has been waiting for your call..."

"Today I am angry on my lucky charm. He was just no help, he was not lucky for me."

"Is that so now? You should punish him then if he is so useless. Why are you wasting your time on such a useless lucky charm?"

"Ok, enough. You have no right to say anything about him. However he is, he is mine. Do you understand that?"

I had a feeling that she was definitely smiling as she said this.

"Come on, I know you can do better than this. A little wider smile, a little more now."

We laughed and I encouraged her to focus on what was coming next rather than lamenting over what had already gone by.

"So have you understood or do you need some more pep talk?"

"Nope, I am fully ready"

"That's like the Aditi I know"

All the remaining exams were really awesome, but we still had the engineering entrance exam – JEE, remaining. It was to take place on 10 April.

It was going to be Aditi's birthday on 11 April. I wanted to make it really special for her, but I had a race against time here. Mom would grill me if I even dared to do anything for Aditi before I got done with the JEE. That left me with just 24 hours to put together whatever preparations I needed for Aditi's birthday.

Nandini Di's wedding was on 15 March, immediately after the exams ended. I was so excited about it. Weddings in my community don't generally take place in the month of March, it is not considered to be very auspicious, but the groom and his family resided in the USA, and they wanted to fly back as soon as they could, and hence, the wedding date was set for March itself.

I wanted to celebrate the end of my Board exams on 14th, but decided against it as mom would feel left out. So I spent the day with mom and my family helping out with the wedding preparations. We cousins had got together again and we had a lot of fun. Mom was the happiest to have me spending time with her. By doing this, I knew I had left Aditi alone, but it was a trade-off I had to make.

So I decided to call on Aditi's once mom was happy that I had given her the importance and the time she deserved, that way I could perhaps keep both the women happy.

I reached Aditi's place at about 10 in the night, she was eating ice cream as she watched an old Hindi movie, wearing her favorite pink pajamas, and all this made her look really cute.

"So finally you got a chance to take out some time for me?"

"I thought we could start the celebrations now. I had to be with mom and help out with the wedding preparations, but I am all yours now, and we can spend as much time as we want together. As it is, your neighbours disturb us a lot in the day. I just didn't want that today."

"Stop it Adi, I know you would have completely forgotten about me. And when it finally clicked you that I might still be waiting for you, you would have rushed to meet me."

"Actually... You are absolutely correct!"

"Adi, I will kill you someday if you ever forget me like this. I will not talk to you now. Continue keeping me forgotten. Go back to your house and sleep."

"And the headlines next day would be 'Lover turns Murderer'... glaring at all the readers right across from the front page!"

"Shut up Adi", she punched me as she said that.

"Sorry, I know that was a bad joke. You asked me to go to sleep, well, I couldn't do that"

"Why, in the name of God, would you be unable to sleep?"

"Someone stole my sleep."

"would you know who the thief is?"

"It is some beautiful princess, always furious with me."

"I am always furious with you? Really? Have you ever noticed what all you do?"

"Who said I was talking about you?"

"Oh please! There is nobody who could tolerate you, but me"

"You really think so?"

"Obviously!! Who do you think can tolerate your poor jokes, and your swinging moods between extremely studious and extremely romantic?"

"But don't I make you laugh too?"

"Yes, but still…"

I did not let her complete, "Then I am doing my job pretty well. My sole aim is to keep that smile fixed on your face at all times. I really don't want anything else in life."

We made our way upstairs to the terrace, it was our favorite place to hang out in her house. We had a lot of memories here. We placed a mat on the ground, and sat down with our backs to the wall. She rested her head on my shoulder, and we looked at the lovely stars in the far off sky.

"Do you know Aditya, now I nothing to worry about. I feel so relieved today. JEE is a little bit tension, but nothing can go wrong when we are together."

"Yes, don't stress off over JEE, take it like just any other exam. So far as we are clear with the basic concepts and fundamentals, there is no stopping us."

"Aditya I just remembered that I wanted to ask you something."

"Shoot"

"When I first came to your house to study, I noticed a pile of books for SAT and TOEFL preparation on your table. …"

After a long pause I said, "You are a keen observer"

"Adi, don't change the topic. Are you planning to pursue your higher education abroad?"

I kept quiet. She got real angry and stood up, "Adi, why did you not tell me about it all this time? We had decided to go to the same college. Now you are also leaving me. You just get up and get out of my house right now. Get up Aditya and leave."

"Aditi calm down, please. They are not my books. They are my cousin, Rony's books. He wants to pursue his higher education in a foreign university. I had bought the books for him, so they could help them achieve his dreams."

"Adi, don't lie to me"

"Aditi, please believe me, calm down"

I hugged her tightly, I hated myself for lying to her. But did I really have an option. I would have to face her someday, but today was not that day, I didn't have the heart to break her heart. I didn't want to lose her.

"The dream" mom always kept talking about was that I wanted to pursue my college degree at the Massachusetts Institute of Technology. This was my dearest dream since I was in 9th grade. But following this dream would distance me from Aditi, and I was not prepared for that. The thought scared me beyond imagination.

15

Changes

We spent the whole night on the terrace. Aditi slept with her head on my shoulder and my arm around her. I kissed her on the forehead, she smiled in response.

I woke up the next morning and did not find Aditi next to me. I called out to her, but she did not respond.. I went downstairs. She was nowhere to be found. I could smell the refreshing aroma of fresh coffee, and ran to the kitchen. There she was, making coffee. She had showered and was fresh as a daisy.

"Coffee for you sir", she said handing me a cup of coffee.

"Aditi I haven't brushed my teeth yet. I will have it sometime later."

"Goodness Adi! it's already 7 in the morning and you have still not brushed your teeth!!!"

"This is way too early for me Aditi, I wake up at nine when I am home"

"Early to bed, early to rise makes a man healthy, wealthy and wise."

"we definitely did not sleep early last night!"

She blushed and said, "Adi don't you get started now! Even when I sleep late, I make it a point to wake up early. When we wake up early we are fresh and happy. A happy morning leads to a happy day. Otherwise, we become pale and lazy, like you are looking right now."

"I am letting you know right now, that even after we get married, I will continue to wake up at 9. I don't buy your happiness theories. I believe food and sleep are two things one must never compromise over"

"Fine! Do what you wanna do. We still have a lot of time before we get married, we are still underage for it."

"I turn 18 this December!"

"I turn 18 in April itself. I am eight month elder to you, and you need to listen to what elders say."

"What do you think have I been doing all this time?"

I kissed Aditi on the cheek after that, and rushed home. It was Nandini di's wedding today. Mr. Desai saw me kissing Aditi, and heard me say, "Bye, love you", as I was wearing my helmet to leave. "Love you too," she said

Mr. Desai was staring at me as if I was a notorious criminal. I ignored him, I was getting really late.. Nandini Di had invited Aditi to the wedding, but it would be alright if she came late. I was her closest cousin and had to be there well before time.

Mom would not knock on my door before 9, she knew I never wake up before that. I reached home and entered from the back door. I slowly made my way to my room and laid down on the bed, acting as if I was still asleep.

Mom came into my room a few minutes after 9. She took out my clothes to wear today from the cupboard and said, "No need to pretend. I know you were not home the whole night. I came to your room last night to tell you how happy I was to see you so happy and enjoying your time with your cousins, but you ruined everything. I understand you wanted to meet her, but it upsets me that you didn't even care to inform me before leaving"

"I thought it would only make you angry if I told you I was going to meet Aditi.."

"So am I not angry right now? Am I not hurt right now? I am your mom, Aditya. How could you even think of fooling me? You thought I will not realize if you slip out of the house in the night thinking I am already asleep? I had realized it the very moment you left when I heard your bike start."

"But mom if I had asked you, you would never have agreed to let me go!"

"Adi, why did you assume I would have refused! Why do you have to think I am your enemy here? I am not. I am your friend and your mother, and I know you love her a lot. I don't like her one bit myself; but I understand our thoughts differ here. And that's ok, we are two different individuals, our choices can be different."

"Mom, I am really sorry. I promise this won't happen again."

"Adi, when we repeat our mistakes, it doesn't remain a mistake, it becomes a habit. It was your responsibility as my son to inform me, I taught you better than this. I feel so sorry right now that you have failed badly at being a son. I don't want to spoil the day anymore, get dressed quickly, we need to reach as early as possible."

My mood was already spoiled, all the excitement was gone. But I couldn't deny that my mom was a lot more open-minded than I gave her credit for. She didn't seem to have any problem that I had spent a whole night with a girl all alone. She had a problem that I did not inform her.

I realized that women are always unpredictable and perhaps the most difficult to understand. Mom's old sarees and grey hair never gave an appearance that she was as open minded as she was. She might have been 42, but she was young at heart and ready to accept the changing mindsets and society.

We rushed to Nandini di's. Everyone seemed busy with the last minute stuff that needed attention. Mom went into the kitchen and started helping my aunts divide the packets of sweets.

All were busy in some or the other work, only I had nothing to do. So I decided to go and meet Nandini Di.

"Chachi I am going upstairs to meet Nandini Di. Is that ok?" I shouted as Chachi was busy outside with some work.

Chachi shouted from outside, "Yes beta, why not. She is alone upstairs as such, Go on, keep her some company, we have to go to the wedding venue in an hour."

"Ok, Chachi." I went to Nandini di's room. She was sitting in front of the mirror, dressed in a beautiful red lehenga. She was looking breathtakingly gorgeous. In my head, I could see Aditi in her. I was imagining the day we would get married.

"Hey, lover boy, still lost in Aditi's thoughts? I am getting married today, I deserve some attention at least!."

"It's not like that di!"

I went close to her and took her hand in mine. "Di, how are feeling. Are you happy? How is Reyansh?"

Reyansh was Nandini Di's husband-to-be. With my board exams on, I hadn't met him yet.

"He is a really nice person. Do I always thought I would fall in love with some handsome guy and marry him, I never thought I would be having an arranged marriage, like I am now.. But we never know on what path destiny takes us. I now realize that whatever happens in life has already been destined to happen, that's our fate and nobody can change it. Reyansh is really the man of my dreams!"

"Seriously di, love changes everything. Don't ever forget that. Do what keeps you happy and always listen to your heart. Life is long, so there will be problems. But don't let the problems break you both; instead let it bring you closer. And then, I am always there for you. If you ever feel you have a problem, call me, I will reach you no matter where you are, I am going to miss you so much!"

I got emotional as I said that. She hugged me and said, "You have really grown up Adi. I am also going to miss you so very much." She went back and asked, "How come you are talking about relation, marriage love, etc, that was never really your, let's say, 'area of interest'..."

"Being in love has also changed me a little Di!"

"Not a little, lover boy, you have changed completely."

16

Sick mindsets

My phone was ringing, it was Aditi. I answered the call and said, "Aditi have some patience, it has not even been an hour since I left your house, and you are missing me already!" She did not reply and started crying. I got worried.

"What is going on Aditi? Stop crying. Please, calm down. I am getting worried now. Please tell me what happened." She did not reply and just hung up the phone.

Hearing me, Nandini Di also got worried. "What happened Aditya? Is everything alright?"

"I don't know Di. Aditi was crying Maybe her aunt is troubling her again"

"You need to go and find out"

"But how can I leave right now. We have to leave for the venue in few minutes. You are getting married today, how I can I leave you?"

"Adi its fine, right now Aditi needs you more than me. I will handle the situation here. Just go fast, she needs you"

"Thanks a lot Di, Love you. I will be back soon."

I quickly slipped out avoiding everybody and rode as fast as I could to Aditi's place.

At Aditi's place, the door was open. I knocked, there was no answer. I entered and called out to her, there was still no answer. I went up to her room, and there she was. She was crying and packing her bags.

"Aditi stop. Please tell me what happened."

I tried holding her hand but she just pushed me away, "Just leave me alone Aditya. Go away."

"Stop it Aditi" I was getting angry now.

"Can you just sit down here" I sat her down on the bed and got her a glass of water from the kitchen. She drank a sip.

"Feeling better now?"

"Yes."

"Now for God's sake will you tell me what is going on here?"

"Aditya the members of the society have asked me to leave the society."

"Why, how can they do that?"

"Adi, because I live alone, and you usually come and stay with me till pretty late in the night. You even stayed all night yesterday. They saw you kissing my good bye this morning. We are not married and we are too young. They said it does not suit our age and that it has a bad effect on their children. They insulted me in front of everyone and told me that such behavior is not acceptable in the society. And I could not do anything, I was really helpless Aditya. I can't live in this society anymore. I should leave this place Adi. They will never understand our relation."

"No Aditi. You are my fighter. You cannot give up like this. We are not wrong, they are. And we need to make them realize their mistake. Every time a young boy and a girl are alone, it doesn't always mean that they are doing something wrong. I know how to teach them a lesson, you wait and see."

"No, Aditya I don't want to create any nuisance."

"No Aditi, it would have been fine if they would have told anything about me; I don't care. But they don't have a right to doubt your character. You just be strong. And give your

Grandfather's will papers. Let's see who stops you from staying in your own house."

Taking the will papers, I went to Mr. Desai's house next door and rang the doorbell Mrs. Desai opened the door.

"Is Mr. Desai home? I wanted to meet him." I said very politely.

"Yes. But who are you?"

"I am Aditya Patel, Aditi's friend."

By now Mrs. Desai knew who I was. She gave me weird looks. I conveniently ignored them. She did not even call me inside. Instead she called Mr. Desai out.

"Oh, so the boyfriend has come to the rescue. I was waiting for you actually"

I was so angry right now, I could have punched his face there. But Aditi held my hand and indicated that I needed to calm down

I very politely said, "Sir these is Aditi's grandfather's will. Legally this house belongs to her. You cannot ask her to vacate it like this."

"Oh, so now you will teach me what I should do. Listen you are just a kid, first grow old enough to argue with me"

"sir, I am being well within my limits and being very polite with you, or else I could…"

"Or else what, what will you do? Ok if I agree that this house belongs to Aditi, then what are you doing in this house. You stay entire nights in the house, are you a tenant? Do you have any legal document to prove that you can stay in this house?"

"No, I don't have any of these."

"See these useless youngsters. I don't know what will happen to this country. When we were of their age we would only focus on studies. And see what all today's generation does. They have no shame and no regret. Have your parents not taught you any manners?"

"Mr. Desai you are taking this too far. Don't bring our families into this. We both come from very respectable families. And neither of us have forgotten any of our values"

"I don't know about you but Aditi's background is not so good. She was thrown out by her own family. I mean just see her; she is not at all shameful for anything she has done so far."

"Enough is enough Sir. Just because we are not saying anything doesn't mean we have done anything wrong that we need to regret. You would be nobody to judge Aditi on her past, you are no one to comment on it. Let me say this again for you, we have not done anything wrong."

"Is sleeping with a girl who is just 17 the right thing to do? Tell me Aditya, is it the right thing to do?"

"Stop it Mr. Desai, just stop it. Our relation is pure, it has no stains. Yes, I did stay with Aditi all night yesterday, but I never even came close to her. We are old enough to understand what is right and what is not, and we very well know where to draw the line. Why is it so difficult for elders like you to accept that? We have not done anything wrong and I don't think I need to give any more explanations."

"Fine! She can stay here. But I don't want this behavior again."

We said nothing and just left. Aditi held my hand and said, "Proud of you!" I was really happy, I had proved to the world that our relation was strong and would not break so easily.

17

The inevitable arguments

I got a bad headache by the time we reached back to Aditi's place. I sat under the fan for a while trying to cool off. My mind was flooded with thoughts. Aditi brought a glass of chilled water for me. It was about 12 noon, Aditi reminded me I had to be at Nandini di's wedding.

"Oh God! How can I forget that? Mom is going to kill me again for this."

She went inside and got dressed in 5 minutes. I told myself, how I could have been the selfish guy to ditch my sister on her wedding! I started my vehicle and we took the shortest route to reach the venue.

Mom saw me and Aditi entering together, the way she looked at us, I can't deny, I was really scared. Luckily, there were still a lot of ceremonies left. Nandini di looked at me and I gave her thumbs up gesture indicating all the best. She said thank you, and asked if everything was fine, without saying a word. I gave her an expression of relief. She smiled, looked towards Aditi and told her that she was looking beautiful. Aditi thanked her and also complimented her.

Women can talk a lot in gestures without saying a word out loud. Nandini Di had seen Aditi for the first time. And I was super excited to know Nandini Di's reaction. Now, I could not go in the middle of the ceremony and ask Di, could I? So I decided to be patient and wait, while mom constantly kept an eye on us, behaving like Sherlock Holmes.

Aditi came close and whispered, "Your sister is really beautiful. You can see the joy of beginning a new phase of life, while there is also some sadness of leaving the family behind. Obviously! Who would want to leave such a cute brother behind" she pulled my cheek as she did this.

"Ms. Aditi Sharma, you are under constant surveillance of your future mother-in-law, you might want to keep some distance!" I pushed her a little away.

"Oh, is aunty here? Where is she? I want to meet her."

"You meet mom now, and we will see the next World War wage out here. Mom has been angry with me since morning for spending the night with you" I said this in my mind.

"I don't think so you would want to meet her now." I said aloud after a while.

"Oh come on. Where is she?"

"Leave it Aditi; she must be really busy right now. You can meet her some other day"

"I wouldn't mind waiting for her, I would really like to meet her today."

"Aditi, don't be stubborn. You want to meet mom, I will take you home one day and you can meet her all you like. Don't disturb her right now, she is furious already"

"Fine! I'll come to your place tomorrow"

"That would be better", I had to agree with her, I couldn't argue with her at the wedding.

We went on to the mandap where the rituals were taking place, and settled on the chairs around.

"You know Aditya sometimes I envy you. You have an understanding mother, beautiful sisters and helpful brothers. Unlike me, your life is complete. I have never known what a loving family means. You are very lucky to be blessed with this."

"You are partly right here. I agree my life is truly complete, but it's because of you and no anybody else. And then, I have to be really lucky to have a soul mate like you. You don't have to envy me, I should be envying you, you have such a loyal, faithful and understanding boyfriend after all. Once we get married, all of my family will always talk about you, and you would have their complete attention; nobody will even ask about me then."

She smiled. And I loved her even more.

The ceremony ended. Nandini Di had gone from being Ms. Nandini Patel to Mrs. Nandini Shah. I realized how difficult it might be for a woman to let go of her identity and take a new, leave her family behind and start a new phase of life amidst strangers. I could not even imagine myself doing that.

I didn't want to let Nandini di go just yet, I wanted her to stay. But, it was time for the vidai rituals, and she had to leave. I hugged her tight, as she was meeting all the family before leaving.

"Di, I will miss you so much. Please don't go, stay with me. With whom will I share my secrets with now?"

"Oh, lover boy! Come on! We are living in the 21st century. We can chat online!"

"Yes, Di of course, we will stay in touch."

"Now listen, listen to what your mom says. Take care of yourself, your mother and Aditi. And don't ever leave Aditi. You both are made for each other. Don't ever hurt her."

"I promise Di, I will never ever leave her."

"And Aditi, Adi is really nice but if ever he hurts you come straight to me. I will take him to task for it. And lastly, guys I will miss you." Nandini Di said hugging us.

Tears rolled down her cheeks. I was also about to cry but I controlled my emotions. Mom, all my aunties, everyone was crying.

Soon di's car arrived and Nandini Di left. I was still digesting the fact that it would be a long, long time before I could see Nandini di again, when everyone went back into the venue and mom walked up towards me. I had no idea what was going to happen and was scared. I definitely didn't have a good feeling about this.

Aditi greeted mom first, "Namaste aunty, how are you?"

Mom ignored her and spoke to me. Aditi felt bad, it showed on her face.

"Aditya I am talking to you. You are getting more and more reckless with each passing day. Where did you suddenly disappear this morning?"

"Mom please, can we discuss this at home. Why are you creating a scene in front of others" I said indicating Aditi was standing next to us.

"Aditya, I don't fear anyone. Who is she that I should be afraid of her and shy away from her? I want to discuss this matter right now, at this very moment in front of everyone." She shouted on me.

I lost my patience and retorted angrily, "Ok, fine discuss whatever you want to discuss. Aditi is mature enough and I am sure she will understand"

"Are you trying to tell me Adi that I do not understand things? That I am not mature enough? I am your mother Aditya, and you are my son, your girlfriend comes later. Or maybe I am wrong, I should forget that you are my son. My son wouldn't disappear at night without informing me and arrive in the morning trying to fool his mom; he wouldn't disappear from his sister's wedding, and he definitely wouldn't argue with me for a girl he has just known a few months. I know I taught my son better. My son always kept family above everything and everybody else."

"Mom please, I have already apologized to you. Could you please forgive me and move on"

"A sorry cannot undo the mistakes you committed Adi. You need to change your attitude right now. And yes Aditi, I don't have any problem with you but you are taking Adi away from us. Adi never behaved so carelessly before. It would be really great if you can stay away from him." She said this and left.

Aditi was shocked, she didn't know how to react to this. She just ran away from there.

"Aditi stop, please listen."

But she did not listen. The whole day had gone in the wedding. It was very late so I worried how Aditi would reach home. I called her multiple times but she never replied to any of my calls or messages. I decided to go to her place and check myself if she had reached safely or not. I reached her home to find the lights on in the living room. I was relieved. For a fleeting moment I thought I should go in and meet her, but I felt she need some time to get over what mom had told her, and then Mr. Desai was also sitting out in the courtyard.

I looked towards and called out, "Just came to see whether she has reached home or not."

Aditi had heard my voice and came to the kitchen window. I saw her and smiled, but she went away. I too started my bike and left.

18

Is everything sorted?

When I reached home Mom was in her room, I was in no mood to meet her, nor did I have the courage to do so. I didn't want to get into another argument with her. Enough bad things and fights had happened through the day, I couldn't take it anymore.

If I knew Aditi as well as I thought I did, she must be feeling guilty and blaming herself for whatever happened today.

But it wasn't her fault, it was nobody's fault. Mom cared for me and couldn't see me giving first priority to someone else. Mom and Aditi both were equally important for me. Mom was finding it difficult to accept that someone else was as important as she was, and I thought maybe it was normal. But wouldn't this happen someday anyways, irrespective of whether Aditi came in my life or not?

But mom had never been so rude to me. The only time she was like this was when she was battling depression. Mom and Dad had met with an accident, that killed my dad and mom incurred a major head injury. She had begun getting panic attacks and was battling acute depression. It took her a few days to get back to normal, but this became a kind of cycle with her. She would be normal for some days and then have frequent panic attacks for the next few days. I had felt so utterly helpless at that time, I didn't know what I could do to help mom get better.

Now if I take Aditi's side, mom gets hurt; if I sided with mom, Aditi takes the hit. I was in a catch-22 situation I knew no way out of. It was getting too confusing and it was draining me out.

I was restless and kept thinking about this all night. I hardly slept. I would stare at the ceiling, I would look out of the window, and Aditi would keep coming back to my mind, again and again. All the time I had spent with her, kept coming back to me. I never realized when I fell asleep, lost in my memories.

The next I was ready to start my day at 8:00. Mom had already left for the school. I sent out a text message to her, "I am going to my friend's house for a while. I will be back before lunch. I had my breakfast. I will also start my JEE preparation in the afternoon after I am back."

She texted back, "I know I don't need to worry about your preparations. I am sure you will do it and crack JEE easily. Call me once you have had your lunch. Love you"

I was shocked at the positive reply, I rubbed my eyes and read it twice. Mom had cheered up, now it was Aditi's turn.

I reached Aditi's place at 8:30 and rang the bell. She opened the door.

"How come are you up so early? Are you for real or am I dreaming"

"You can believe what you want, but for a person who begins her day at 7, 8:30 is far from early."

"It's early for you, don't you have a habit of waking up at 9?"

"Well I couldn't manage staying away from you anymore so decided to drop by"

"I don't believe you, there must be something, you won't wake up early for nothing"

"It's interesting to see the Sherlock Holmes side of you. But it might be more interesting if you could let me in and then continue your investigation"

"Oh yeah, come on in"

I pulled her closer and looked straight into her eyes. I tucked her hair behind her ear, when we smelt something burning.

Aditi pushed me away and ran into the kitchen. I followed suite.

"Goodness! I kept milk on the stove to boil and forgot all about it!"

She turned the stove off in a rush.

"It's ok, people tend to forget things when I am around, they get so lost in my charm…"

"Aditya this is cheating, come on! This is unfair"

"What did I do in that?"

She remained silent and blushed a little.

"Aditi, are you alright?"

"Yes Adi, totally, why? Was something supposed to happen to me?"

"Aditi don't feign innocent. I am talking about yesterday and you know that."

"Adi, I know Aunty was angry, there must be a reason for it. She would always have our best interests at heart. Your mom has no one but you, and it is natural for her to be possessive and bit insecure about you like she was yesterday"

"So you are not at all angry?"

"No Adi of course not"

I was so relieved, I hugged her tight for this.

"Why did you not come in last night? You were right outside"

"I thought you might have been angry and upset and that I should give you some time to get a grip and calm down."

"No Adi, it's nothing like that. I was really angry for a moment, but when I looked at things from her perspective, it made sense. It was just a bad day Adi, and it led to all the chaos. Let's not think about it so much"

"Oh Aditi I am so lucky to have you in my life!"

19

Special Days

L ife went on. After a little break again everything was falling back to normal. We worked really hard preparing for JEE. We did not study long hours, but once books were in our hand, we thought of nothing but what was in the book.

The days seemed to pass pretty quickly. The night before the exam Aditi called me. She was nervous as usual.

"Adi, I am really worried. I have never taken such exams. What will happen tomorrow?"

"Don't worry Aditi. You are unnecessarily stressing yourself out. We have worked really hard for this and we will rock the exam tomorrow."

"I just hope everything goes well"

"Relax. Think about day after tomorrow. It's your first birthday which you will celebrate with me. Think of how special it will be, keep guessing what gift I will give you."

"Adi with you every day is special for me."

"Are you trying to distract me before the exam? Is that your plan?"

"I am trying to be romantic and you are disappointing!"

"If you were half as disappointed as you say you are, you wouldn't have that wide bright smile stuck on your face!"

"How do you always find out Adi!"

The exam went well, it was finally over. We were free now, we could enjoy and celebrate to our heart's fill.

It was Aditi's birthday tomorrow and I had so many things in my mind and I had barely 24 hours to put all that in place. I couldn't figure where to start the preparations. This seemed even more difficult than preparing for the exams.

Aditi had been calling me and texting me ever since we came out of the exam hall, but I was just not responding to any of it. I had a 100 texts from her in under 3 hours. She must have been really desperate to talk to me and meet up, but I wanted to surprise her the next day and continued preparing for the big day.

Once I had completed everything to my satisfaction, I asked mom "Mom tomorrow is Aditi's birthday. Would it ok if I go and wish her at night. It is her first birthday that we would be celebrating together. Please mom, I promise you I won't irresponsible and I will come home as soon as possible. Please Mom, please mom, please."

"Ok, Adi you can go but come home as soon as possible."

I felt life would be a lot less complicated if I took mom in confidence and remained honest with her, and it worked!

I reached Aditi's house at 11:45 pm. She might have retired for the day, she took her own sweet time to open the door.

"Adi, what are you doing so late here? The neighbors could see us and we would be in so much trouble, you know that? Go home. You haven't answered any of my calls or texts all day, I am not talking to you anywhich ways. Just go home"

"Aditi can we play the angry game later, I am in a little rush here. Can I come in now?"

"No Adi you don't get to come in"

"Aditi you are wasting time" I was losing patience. My hands were tired with holding so many things, so I pushed her away and got in anyways. I apologized to her on my way in, "Sorry for this one, just stay here, ok?"

I ran to the terrace. I set up the projector to face the plain wall at the door to terrace. I lit the candle on the birthday cake. I turned around to check everything was in place and ran downstairs! I held her hand and brought her upstairs. It was dark all around, the only light was that of the projector and the candle.

"I love you Aditi Sharma, I love you more than anybody else in this world. I promise I will never leave you"

I had made a movie of all our pictures that we had captured and it started playing behind us on the projector. It showed all the memories we had had in the past 8 months. Each picture had a voice over from me describing what it stood for, and the story behind each picture.

Aditi was stunned. I held up the cake for her, "A very Happy Birthday Aditi! May you live long and happy!"

She did not let me complete, "I want to spend all my life with you" She hugged me tight.

"I am not going anywhere Aditi, I will always be there in your heart"

She cut the cake and was about to offer it to me when I said, "Tell me, who do you think is sweeter - The cake or the person who baked the cake?"

"Ummmm… Let's clear the confusion!"

She fed me the piece.

"It's tough competition but I think the cake is sweeter. The cake has to be sweeter than the person who made it after all!, but Adi, you actually baked the entire cake on your own for me?"

"Yes of course!"

"It's awesome. It's just so delicious"

I swelled with pride, "But I am still sweeter than you"

"Yeah, of course Adi, that's because you are with me!?"

She started hitting me playfully, and I ran while she followed me downstairs. .

"Ok Aditi don't get violent on this special day. I agree that you are 1/3rd as sweet as me? Is that ok?" I said running.

"I am only 1/3rd sweet! Really? You better run fast, I won't spare you this time!"

I reached the living room and slowed down. Aditi caught up with me and we faced each other.

"Come on, you want to see my bitter side, come on!" She pushed me backwards on the couch and I held her, she fell on top of me. She continued complaining.

She was quiet a while later and our eyes met. We came closer and I tucked her hair behind her ears. We closed our eyes and kissed each other. I pulled her closer, it was our first kiss.

Sometime later, we came back to our senses. She tried getting up but couldn't as I held her down. I let her go and we sat up on the couch. We didn't know what to say, it was getting a little awkward.

"I think I should go and get the cake from upstairs and shut down the projector"

"Yes"

I could not believe what had just happened.

I heard Aditi call out from downstairs, "You have received some emails, is it alright if I check them? "Adi someone is constantly sending you email. Your mobile is ringing since a long time, can I check it, it might be urgent..."

"Of course Aditi, go on. Let me know if it is anything important"

"Ok."

After a while she called out, "Nope, nothing important. Ronit has sent some links for some games."

I continued packing things on the terrace.

20

Fairytale turned nightmare

As I went downstairs, Aditi was crying, my phone in her hand. I ran up to her and asked, "What happened Aditi, why are you crying? Is everything ok?"

"Aditya, are you not telling me something?"

"No, Aditi I have not hidden anything from you, I have told you everything and been completely honest with you."

"Aditya stop lying. Are you sure there is nothing you should have told me, like long ago?" she said this one out really loud.

"Aditi calm down. Please. Listen to me…"

"Aditya, yes or no?"

"Yes Aditi, there is something I haven't told you but I should have. I had applied in to the Massachusetts Institute of Technology, it has been my dream to study there since I was in 9th grade. They really seemed to like my portfolio. I never told you this because I was afraid I would lose you, I was scared you would assume that I was going to leave you and go away like everyone else did. But that's not how it really is. I will be gone for just 4 years, and then I will come running back…", this only made her angrier and she threw my phone away, so much that the screen cracked and the cover and battery came away.

"And when were you planning to tell me about this Aditya? After you reached the US? Good news for you then, they have called you for an interview. You have what you want now? Happy? No one has ever hurt me the way you have, Aditya. It was such a mistake to get involved with you and have expectations of you. I thought you were different but I was so wrong. All people are actually just the same, I was so wrong to believe otherwise. Now I understand why your mom was so upset with you, because you just assume how people will respond while you continue doing your own thing without bothering about others. That is what you did with your mother and that is what you doing to me now. And I like an idiot could not see such a simple thing, it was staring right at me all this time. Had you told me that this was your dearest dream, I wouldn't have been an obstacle for you, I would have happily supported you. I thought today would be the happiest day of my life, but you disappointed me, and you broke my heart. Today, I regret every single moment I have spent with you. You never thought I could be an understanding partner and supported your dreams. You should have been the one telling me about this Aditya, I shouldn't have had to find out about this through an email. Let me make this easier for you, you don't have to leave me anymore, I leave you, forever. I don't want to see you anymore, I don't want to talk to you anymore. Leave my house this very moment"

Aditi was saying the very same words mom had some time back. I was so happy with Aditi, I didn't want to leave her. I didn't know what to do.

She kept shouting and crying, and pushed me out of the house. Her loud voice had woken up the whole neighbourhood by now, and everybody was out on the road, staring at me being thrown out of house.

There Mr. Desai was, telling anybody who would listen, "Sometime back this boy was giving me speeches on true love. And now look at him and his love!"

I chose to ignore him. Did I have an option? I sat outside and kept staring at the door, long after Aditi had shut it behind me. Why did this have to happen today, why? I had tried so hard to make the day special for Aditi, and I had ruined it all. I broke into tears, and I sat on the steps to Aditi's house and kept crying for a long time. I was trying to save our relationship looking for the right moment and I had only ruined it in the process. I was shattered. I had never felt this pain. Mom was right, love is just as painful as it is beautiful.

Sometime later after I had poured my heart out in my tears, I got a grip on myself and got up. I decided I couldn't let her go so easily, I really, really loved her after all. I would have to wait for a while for things to cool down, but I would not give up. I decided to wait, and prepare myself to face her again. I walked towards my bike, and looked up at the terrace. She was standing there, looking at me with all those pain and agony in her eyes. Neither of us was happy. I so wanted to hold her and tell her that I would never go away from her, I couldn't live without her, that I could never live without her. But in this moment, she wouldn't be able to understand. I put on my helmet and just rode away. I didn't know where I was going, I didn't know where I wanted to go. At the next crossroads, I had almost got hit, but the car braked at the last moment and was saved. The car driver abused me angrily and drove off. I was lost, I didn't think I could drive anymore. I parked on the roadside and sat on a bench. I had broken Aditi's heart, but my own heart was broken too. I was trying to put off something, afraid I was lose her, and by doing just that, I had lost her. I had so many dreams that I wanted Aditi to be a part of, I wanted a lifetime of being with her. I still couldn't accept it that I had lost her. I was trying to keep some hope alive, but it was dark all around in my heart, rays of hope couldn't really be there.

While I was still wiping my tears off, I realized I had spent the night on the roadside bench. Dawn was already past, the sun was just about to rise. I realized mom would be waiting for me at home. It was time to gather myself together and go home.

I reached home to find the door locked from outside. Mom used to leave for school at about 7, it was just about 6:30. I reached out for my phone in my pocket and remembered the fate my phone had met with last night.

"Damm it!" I punched the door.

I opened the door, and foolishly kept looking for mom from room to room, realizing much later that if the door was locked from outside, mom definitely wouldn't be home.

I picked up the landline phone and dialed into mom, she did not reply. I tried again, and then again. Finally, on the third attempt, she answered my call.

Before she could say anything, I began, "Mom where are you? I have been looking for you!. I was so worried for you. Mom you were so right. Love is really painful, I cannot handle this pain anymore. I need to see you mom, where are you?"

"Hello, Aditya; good morning to you too!"

I heard a man's voice, this was not mom.. I double checked the number I had dialed only to find that I had dialed correctly. But if the person knew my name, chances are I might know him too. My brain just wasn't working.

"Who is this?" "Hello, Aditya I am your neighbor, Mr. Nagar."

"Uncle how come you are answering my mother's phone?"

"You should come to the Bhailal Amin Hospital, quickly. Your mom has been admitted here, we have been trying to reach you all night."

I hung up, grabbed my wallet, locked the door and rushed to the hospital on my bike. I could see mom all sick and in pain. I was guilty, stressed, worried and depressed. That makes a deadly cocktail of disaster.

21

The stubborn fate

I reached the hospital and asked at the reception. "Can you please tell me what room is Mrs. Falguni Patel?"

Before the receptionist could answer Mr. Nagar came over, "Aditya, we were so worried. Where were you?"

"Uncle where is mom? What happened to her"

"Go straight, turn left and she is in the first room."

I literally ran towards the room avoiding crashing into someone or something. I didn't even ask the doctor if I could visit mom, I just pushed the door and walked in. I was so desperate to see her, to know that she was alive and alright.

She was unconscious. She lay on the bed absolutely still. I wanted to talk to her, I wanted to apologize for leaving her alone and going away. I was lost in my own world when she needed me so badly.

"Mom please, I need you. Please talk to me."

She couldn't hear me, she hardly moved. The doctor walked in and asked me, "Who are you? And what are you doing here?"

"Doctor, I am her son. How is she? What happened to her? Will she be alright?"

"She is fine. You should go out now, she needs to rest. She kept asking for you all night, she wanted to talk to you. Come, let's go outside"

We both went out. "Please tell me what happened doctor"

"Did you mom incur any major injuries in her past?"

"Yes doctor, when I was around four, my parents had met with an accident. My dad died in it, while my mom incurred a diffuse axonal injury."

"Oh that's quite severe but that explains her panic attacks. She was admitted here last night with a very high fever, and her treatment was difficult as she kept having multiple panic attacks. People who have had head injuries in the past often suffer from stress disorders, depression, panic attacks and anxiety in their future life. Your mom must be having a severe headache due to these. That pain can get really unbearable at times. Something of the sort must have happened last night. Tell me, is she a patient of Dysthymia?"

I gave her a clueless look, I had no idea what that meant.

"Dysthymia means chronic depression."

"Yes, she is."

"Has she ever complained of headaches?"

"No, she never has"

"People usually take headaches quite lightly. You have nothing to worry about; your mother should gain consciousness by today evening. We would like to keep her under observation for the night, then you can take her home in the morning."

Mom had never complained about anything. She never grumbled about her health, or money or any other thing. Maybe it was because she wasn't the complaining person or maybe I never had time to listen to her complaints. In order to be happy in my world, I had left her far too behind, I had disconnected from her.

My maternal uncle, Raghu uncle, came running towards me. He stopped in front of me and slapped me hard.

"Where were you the whole night? You are such a disappointment, I expected better out of you. I let Falguni live alone because I trusted you that you would care for her and be there for her. But you are such an irresponsible guy..."

All the emotions I had venting up inside me so far came gushing out, "Yes I am irresponsible. I am the worst son and the worst boyfriend you will ever meet. I am tired of being a good and an obedient kid. I am tired of saving each and every relation. All this is just so exhausting. Aditi asked me to get out of her life last night. How can I do that, when she is my life? And now mom is in the hospital, again because of me. Anything bad that happens is because of me. I am the bad luck. So go on, slap me again, I so deserve it. But no, I don't serve to be slapped by you, only mom or Aditi are allowed to do that. They are in what shape they are right now because of me. And if you were so concerned about mom, then where were you last night? Why come now? You should have come last night itself. I am cent percent sure Nagar uncle would have called you last night. Do you have anything to say on that?"

My life was getting more and more drama, it was becoming a living nightmare and it was so exhausting. I ran outside the hospital. I was just going to start my bike and drive off, where, I hadn't decided.

But I realized mom needed me, running away from the situation wouldn't help. Raghu uncle was standing in the corridor just as I had left him. He had never seen this ugly side of me, he had only known me as the soft and shy Aditya.

"I was disturbed and stressed out, I am sorry I was rude to you", I apologized to uncle.

"I am guilty of not being here too"

I spent the entire day at the hospital, I hadn't eaten anything since the previous night. My eyes were red and puffy with lack of sleep. I was getting more and more restless I was pacing around impatiently, but mom was far from gaining consciousness. I was pestering the doctor and the nurse every time saw them, asking them if mom was going to be alright. They asked me to calm down and wait. I waited and waited and waited.

At 8 in the night, the doctor came out of mom's room after checking up on her and told me, "She is fine and awake fine now. We will keep her under observation tonight. Tomorrow morning you can take her home. You can go and meet her now"

"Thank you doctor, thank you so much"

I pushed open the door and smiled at seeing her awake again. I held her hand and kissed her forehead. She was really weak.

She left my hand, "I don't have the energy to argue with you right now, but let me get better and then I will talk to you"

"Mom, please don't do this. I am really very sorry. I know my mistake. This time, I swear it was beyond my control"

"Shut up Adil don't' want to talk right now"

"Mom please try and understand. You don't know what I am going through."

"Do you know what I was going through. I was suffering and in pain all alone at home. There was nobody to support me. What good is having a grown up son if he can never be there even when his mother so badly needs him? I called you a hundred times. You never answered even one of them. All of this because of that Aditi! Why won't you just throw her out of your life?. She brings bad luck wherever she goes. She has made you so careless and irresponsible"

She was losing her temper, and began shivering. I did't what was happening to her. I ran outside and called the doctor. He asked me to go outside.

As I went out I could feel Aditi was around. I ignored the feeling, my mind as playing games with me.

The doctor gave mom some injections to calm her down. He came out and told me, "She can't take any stress right now. It's not good for her health. Try to steer clear of everything that would stress her out"

"Yes, doctor I will take care."

22

Time for some atonements

In 24 hours, I had got disconnected and separated from the two women I loved the most in my life. Until last night, I was the reason to live for both of these women and now 24 hours later, both of them wanted a future without me in it. I sat outside mom's room and felt ashamed of myself, of what I had done to both. I wanted to see both of them happy all the time, and I myself ruined their happiness.

A nurse walked up to me and asked me if I was Aditya Patel.

"Yes, I am Aditya"

"Someone called Aditi Sharma had come to see you. I gave her directions to your mother's room and told her that she would find you here. She came here and left, and asked me to give you this"

In one moment, I had gone from feeling ashamed and shattered to feeling hopeful and elated. Aditi had come here to visit mom and me!

"Did she say anything else?"

"No sir, nothing else. She was a little disturbed, but she didn't say anything else"

The nurse left and I opened the box that Aditi had asked her to give me. It had my phone inside, repaired and working again.

It was 9 in the night and I remembered that it was still Aditi's birthday, there were three more hours to go for the day to end. I called her from the phone she had returned. As I could hear the ring, it hit me! How did Aditi know where I was?

As Aditi answered the phone, I said, "Hello Aditi! Happy Birthday! How are you? Thanks for the phone. I appreciate it. I am really sorry for all that happened, and I don't know what to do that you could forgive me. How did you know where I was?"

There was no response from her end. I continued.

"It's ok if you don't want to talk, I understand you are angry. Then shout on me, get your anger out on me, but don't go silent on me. Please say something! Please talk to me!"

I think I heard a sob, and then she hung up. I hadn't let her cry in eight months, and then I ruined it all on her birthday! She hadn't cried all this time because of me, and now she was crying because of me.

All the pain was venting up inside me and I so wanted to let it out. I so desperately wanted to talk to someone. Earlier, Nandini di was always there, but now she had her own married life and I didn't want to disturb her. But I couldn't think of anyone else. It was 11 in the night for me, it was 1:30 in the afternoon for her. I decided to take my chances and called her. And she picked up my phone immediately.

"Hi Adi, how are you? I miss you so much. How is aunty? And how is Aditi?"

I could not say anything, not a word.

"Adi, is everything alright?"

I broke into sobs and tears.

"Adi, please stop crying and tell me what happened"

I slowly told her the whole story interjected by my sobs. She listened quietly.

"Adi, this time it is your mistake. But you had no control over chachi's health. It's just the situation that was wrong. As for Aditi, what you did was completely wrong"

"I know Di; and I realize that. But what should I do now? I just don't know what to do"

"Listen Adi, Aditi really loves you a lot. She cannot live without you. Maybe you should give her sometime, and things will be alright eventually"

"Di, she came to meet me in the hospital, but did not enter the room. She got my phone repaired and gave it to the nurse to hand over to me. I called her back, she answered the phone but didn't say a word"

"Don't worry Adi. She came to meet you. At least that means there is some hope. Don't lose hope Adi. Don't give up so soon. But don't forget about chichi either. You have to be really careful. Chachi and Aditi both need you. You have to balance them both in your life and give them equal time and attention."

"Di I have not been able to do that, I am scared now

"Don't get scared Adi, this is just how things are, and you will have to work your way with it. It is a tough job, but you can't afford to ignore either Aditi or chachi. You know hat makes them happy and you know both are short tempered. It is a difficult task, but this is the path you have chosen for yourself or maybe destiny chose it for you. Chachi has been battling depression and has nobody but you, Aditi has gone through a lot at a very young age and she also has nobody but you. There will be times when one or both of them will be cross with you, then you need to stay calm and not lose your cool. Don't argue with them, don't fight with them. Take it easy and cool. And then I am always there with you. If there is any problem I will come there and try to sort it out."

"Di it's such a relief talking to you. You always know how to calm me down. Di, promise me, no matter what happens you will always remain with me like this." "Of course I am there for you dear. I will always be with you. You must be tired now, you have had a long day. Go, get some sleep, you need it."

"Yes, Di. Love you and miss you a lot."

"Love you to lover boy. Bye"

It felt so much better after talking to Nandini di, all of my emotions had come out and I felt so much lighter now. I fell asleep on the chairs outside mom's room itself.

The next morning mom was looking much better and fresher. In fact, I was look a lot more dull and pale compared to her. The nurse brought in the discharge papers, we signed them and finished the formalities. We went home and I accompanied mom to her room. She lied down on her bed.

"Mom, you take some rest, I will go have a quick shower"

She stopped me and said, "Adi, eat something first. I am sure you wouldn't have eaten anything since yesterday"

I was happy that she showed concern, maybe she was forgiving me and coming back to normal.

"Don't worry mom, I will have something. You get some rest, I will be back soon, I am right here."

I went to take a shower. Mom was fine now, and I was still concerned about Aditi; I didn't know if she was fine or not. I wanted her back, I wanted things to go back to the way they were before

I came out of the shower, put on my clothes and was ready to start a new day, I wore Aditi's favorite cobalt blue deep neck t-shirt. I went downstairs and decided to cook something. I googled some good breakfast recipes and settled for Rava Upma. I hadn't cooked it before, and I was afraid I would burn it all. But fortunately nothing like that happened.

I took the upma out in a plate and took it mom's room in a tray.

"Fresh, hot rava upma is ready for you ma'am!" I said as I entered mom's room. Mom was super happy seeing this. "I would like to fall sick more often if I am going to be treated like this"

"Mom I can treat you like this whenever you want. You don't have to fall sick for it."

"Adi, it's really nice."

"Thank you. I am your son after all, I had to be as close to perfect as I could"

"Yes, you are my son, you have to be perfect."

We both laughed. I was so happy seeing Mom happy. I was careful not to bring up the topic of Aditi even vaguely.

"Mom, MIT really liked my profile and they are seeking and interview with me. I need to go to a cyber cafe to complete the procedure. I could do it at home, but the internet speed is really bad these days. Would you be alright, I will be back soon?"

"Yes, of course I will be fine. I am so happy they liked your profile! Go get the procedure done, but come back soon"

"Yes, Mom I promise I won't be late, I really mean it this time" She smiled and I smiled back.

What I could not tell her, was that I was going to meet Aditi. She was not supposed to talk or think about anything that would stress her out. I didn't like doing it, but I had to lie to her. I promised myself in my head that I won't do it again.

23

What's happening?

I reached Aditi's home in 10 minutes. I was worried as I did not know how she would react. I took a deep breath, gathered all my courage and rang the bell.

She opened the door. She was happy as she saw and then her smile faded away, the sadness came back. I could she see wanted to hug me happily and invite me in, but her mind wouldn't let her do it. I dare not step closer to her or touch her in any way. We just kept looking at each other. She left the door open and went in. I walked in behind her. She kept her back to me and refused to face me.

"Aditi stop it. We have to face this some or the other day. Let's talk about it"

"I don't want to talk about anything Adiyta. Just leave me alone."

"No Aditi you are wrong. Don't lie to me. I know you are a pathetic liar"

"Aditya, I don't want to talk to you. Don't you understand?"

"Stop it Aditi. If you did not want to talk anything why did you come to meet me in the hospital yesterday?"

"I just came to return the phone."

"Oh, come on Aditi if you just had to return my phone you would not have come till Mom's room. You could have left it at the reception itself"

"Aditya stop behaving as if you know everything about and can predict and interpret my behavior"

"What do you mean Aditi? Should I act as if we are strangers; what do you want me to do?"

"You have already done what you had to do, you better not do anything more"

"Aditi I have apologized for that. And here, I apologize again. I am really very sorry Aditi. I was scared of losing you. I am not able to handle this pain anymore. I know I should have told you and I promise you that this will never happen again. Please forgive me, I am really sorry"

"Stop all this nonsense Aditya."

"You stop it Aditi. Come on I can see the pain in your eyes. Tell me you don't want to keep this relation anymore. Look at me and tell me you don't want me in your life anymore"

"Aditya I don't need to do anything, I have nothing to prove. I have made my decision and that is final. I won't change my mind, if that is what you are trying to achieve and hoping for"

"Aditi, I never thought you could lose hope so easily. Tell me you didn't come to talk to me and mend things last night?"

"Aditya leave"

"Just answer me yes or no?"

"Fine! If that's what you want to hear, I came to the hospital last night to mend things, better? Will you leave now?"

"Then what's the problem, Aditi? Now I have come to sort it. So, why do you not want to do it anymore?"

"Aditya, will you leave now or should I call the neighbors?"

"Aditi what is wrong with you?"

"You don't need to understand anything. Just leave"

"Aditi please, I beg of you"

"Aditya, this is the last time I am telling you. Get out of my house right now. Don't ever try to meet me or contact me in any way ever again. I don't want to see your face ever again"

"Ok I will go. I have just one last question. Who told you that I was in the hospital? Tell me that, and I will leave"

"I went to your house to return the phone, but it was locked. So I asked your neighbors, but Nagar uncle and aunty both were not home, only their kids were home. They told me that your mom was not well and had been taken to the hospital."

Aditi was being totally unpredictable. I was upset and angry. I know she had forgiven me for what I had done then why was she behaving like this? Aditi was behaving in a way she never had before. I was really very angry. How could she do this to me? Why was she behaving like this? She was behaving really weird. Something was still bothering her but I couldn't put my finger on it.

I returned home to find mom waiting for me. There were two people in the living, neither of whom I knew even vaguely, while mom was in the kitchen.

"Mom I told you not to get up from your bed. You are still weak and the doctor has asked you to take rest. You are not going to do any work for the next whole week. Go sit outside, then go back to bed"

"Ok, Ok fine I am going, you give them water, and come quickly, I have a surprise for you."

I smiled at her. I poured water from the jug into the glasses, went outside and offered it to the guests.

"Adi, we have now taken a Wi-Fi modem. Now you can have 24 hours internet access at great speed. I have taken the unlimited plan so you can use as much as you want."

"Wow, Mom that's great. This is really very useful. Now I can complete the entire admission procedure sitting right here at home."

"And I have another surprise for you"

"Really?" I sat wide eyed, wondering what it would be

"Yes, of course"

"It seems like it's my lucky day today"

"Last week I had ordered a mobile for you from Flipkart, your new iPhone 6 has just arrived"

I gave mom a tight hug, I was so happy. Mom had been so nice and gave me something I so dearly wanted

"Ok, Adi this is too much love for one day."

"Mom, you have really made my day today. You are really the best Mom in this world."

After the delivery boy and the internet connection people had left, I said, "Mom, don't you think this is too expensive. How will we manage?"

"You don't have to worry about that. Your father and I had saved enough well before you were born, to be able to fulfill your wishes now. And then, when have you ever asked for anything. I haven't been able to give you a birthday gift in the past 3-4 years, you never accept it. Take this as a collective present of all these years. The Americans would laugh on you if they see the mobile you carry right now."

"Ok Ma'am as you say!"

Mom's health was improving and I was trying to spend as much time as I could with mom. I had nobody else to visit or meet, so mom had my undivided attention. Aditi never wanted to see me again, so it was no good pushing her again. I would keep thinking about her and get restless, but I kept calm for mom's sake. Mom was still recovering, she hadn't really recovered completely. She was still battling depression, had panic attacks and severe mood swings.

I kept myself busy with other things and focused on the admission procedure to MIT. I had asked for a concession for being unable to make it to the interview in-person due to mom's ill health and had requested them to consider my application via a video conference interview. They had accepted the same, I had outstanding SAT and TOEFL grades to thank for that. I didn't want to leave mom alone just yet.

The interview went very well. I could see they were really impressed. I told myself not to jump to conclusions and make assumptions.

The results were to be announced two days later.

I would keep staring at Aditi's number, but never really come around to dialing it. I tried keeping myself busy and distracted, but Aditi was on my mind all the time. I did not have any other good friends I could talk to or hang out with. My life had always revolved around mom before Aditi came in, and whenever I wanted to talk to someone, it was always Nandini di.

24

Holding on...Letting go

Finally it was the day the results would be announced. I kept checking my MIT account and refreshing the page on my phone. All the updates were going to be released into our MIT login accounts where we had created our profiles for application to the institute.

It was almost evening, still no results. I was super worried, and pacing all over the house

"Adi, don't worry. The results will come today and I am sure you will make it" Mom was trying to calm me down but it wasn't helping. I had never been so worried even before taking any of the exams. I had really worked hard and didn't want to fail. And then I had paid a really very high price to get into the institute, I couldn't afford to lose it now.

At 7:43 in the evening, my phone beeped and the much awaited message came.

Mr. Aditya Patel,
Congratulations!
We are pleased to inform you that you have successfully cleared all the examinations and interview conducted by Massachusetts Institute of Technology.

You have successfully secured an admission to the Massachusetts Institute of Technology in Mechanical engineering stream ....

The e – mail went on. I read it three times. Mom came from her room, saw me reading the e-mail with eyes wide open. I was sitting on the sofa and she stood behind me.

"Mom I did it" I said really softly.

"Why you are so low, Aditya you got the admission!" She was way more excited than I was. I turned around and hugged her, mom had tears in her eyes.

"Mom, don't cry. This is something we should celebrate. Come, let's go out for dinner today"

Mom nodded her head and smiled over the tears.

"Adi, when does the term start? When are you supposed to report to the institute?"

"I have to be there by 8 June"

"So we just have about a month to prepare"

"Yes mom"

I wanted to share the news with Aditi but I was hesitant to call her. Will she answer my phone? Will she still be angry? Maybe she will ask me not to call her ever again. That was ok, I was so desperate to hear her voice! I thought, how bad could it to be, and finally dialed her number. It went unanswered. The next time I tried, her phone was switched off.

I just didn't understand Aditi. It spoilt my mood, screwed the happy feeling I had for getting the admission. I had to give up on Aditi to achieve my dreams, that was too steep a price to pay.

I was in no mood to go out after what happened when I tried to call Aditi. But I had asked mom already and didn't want to ruin her mood I had lost Aditi, I didn't want to lose mom too.

I took mom to my most favorite restaurant. Mom was making suggestions on what to order, and I was just nodding my head, I had no idea what she was saying, my head was lost in Aditi's thoughts.

As my reverie broke, I looked up from the menu to the table in front of me. Was I still day-dreaming or was it really Aditi sitting there all by herself. It really was Aditi.

Mom hadn't seen Aditi so far as she had her back to her, Aditi hadn't seen me either as she was still going through the menu deciding what to order.

As she looked up from the menu, she saw me. I wanted to just take her hand and run away to some far off land where there would be no one else. I smiled at her. She got up and left.

I pretended I had a call and told mom I didn't have a good signal reception inside, and went outside on that pretext. I caught up with Aditi in the parking lot.

"Aditi stop". She didn't stop and kept walking. I called out to her again.

"You have no right to tell me what to do and what not to"

"Aditi can you please tell me what has happened to you?"

"Aditya you know it very well, making me say it all over again won't change what you did"

"Aditi, I really don't know what's wrong with you?"

"Aditya what part of don't ever meet me again did you not understand?"

"I didn't come here to meet you Aditi, stop behaving like everything has to be about you and tell me what happened"

"Adi stop now."

"Did you call me Adi? You can call me Adi and I can't even ask you to stop? You are just great!"

"It's not like that"

"Then what is it? Please explain, because I am unable to understand anything? You come to my favorite restaurant, you call me Adi and still don't want to talk to me and see me, and that you don't love me anymore!"

"Aditya I did not come here because of you, I came here for myself"

"Oh, really? I don't think so. Fine, you didn't come to this restaurant because you were missing me or because it is my favorite restaurant, But if you came to the hospital to sort things out, then why have you been refusing to do that all this time?"

"I don't think I need to answer any of your questions", she said this and walked away.

I blocked her way, held her arms down and said, "This is not fair Aditi, you need to answer my questions. You cannot leave like this" I was really angry.

She kept her head down and broke into tears. I pulled her closer and held her. She pushed me away and walked off.

"We cannot be together Adi, we are just not meant to be together". This was all she said as she ran away from me, crying.

"Aditi please stop!"

But she did not stop. She left me all alone again. She was also going through the same pain I was.

I went back to Mom. Our food just arrived. We had our dinner and went back home.

I could not sleep that night. I went out to the balcony to get some fresh air. After the hot day, the cool nights were a lot of relief. I took a deep breath. The hotel incident was playing again and again in my mind.

That night I decided not to meet or contact Aditi again. But I knew one day, she would still come back to me.

25

One last time

The month was coming to an end, my passport, visa and tickets were ready. I was ready to begin a new phase of my life. I was ready to realize my dream. But I had an old account to settle, I couldn't begin a new without doing that. I had some hope left inside me that maybe, just maybe Aditi and I could still get back together. I still didn't know what was bothering her. I had tried calling her so many times, I had sent so many texts. She hadn't answered any of them. I had stopped trying to reach her after the restaurant incident though. I was finally tired of chasing her and begging her to talk to me, I was eager to put this all behind me in a few days and begin a new life. I was tired of mom's mood swings and depression. I was just tired of everything.

I still tried to show that I was happy. I had my flight on 6 June. I would go to Mumbai from Vadodara and from there I would board my flight to Cambridge. I was booked into a Jet Airways flight from Vadodara to Mumbai and then onwards, I was flying Lufthansa.

I was excited to have fulfilled my dream. I had worked really hard to balance my Board exams, the SAT and TOEFL; and I had succeeded in doing that. All those hours and hours of hard work, had yielded result. But my personal life had taken a toll for it. I kept pretending and behaving as if she meant nothing to me anymore, that I had forgotten her, but actually I hadn't. I failed to realize why when she had wanted to mend things did she still throw me out of her life. I kept telling myself that if she has stopped caring then so should I, that I should forget her and focus on my future. I told myself hat I tried everything I could. I apologized to her, I tried to talk to her. But she didn't want to do it anymore. I didn't know of any other way to make her realize that I still loved her ad wanted her to remain in my life. Nandini di told me the same thing when I was talking to her one day.

"Yes, Di I have tried very hard. You are right I should concentrate on what is going to happen rather than thinking on what has already happened."

"Now that's like my brother! Best of luck Adi, I am sure you are going to rock it"

I had called Nandini di on the morning of the 5th. It was my last day in Vadodara. I was very restless that night. I had an early morning flight the next day. I wanted to talk to Aditi, I didn't want to leave without meeting her once. I wanted her to know how much I loved her.

I got up, changed into my jeans and grabbed my bike keys. Mom was still awake.

"Mom I am not able to sleep, can I just take a round and come back. I need some fresh air. It might make me feel a bit better"

"Ok, but you have to wake up early so come back soon"

"Yes, Mom I will be back soon. My phone will always be on, so if anything happens call me immediately"

"Ok"

I left to meet Aditi one last time. I was dying to see her. I reached her place and impatiently rang the bell three- four times. She opened the door. She was wearing her favorite pink pajamas. I was so happy to see her that I could not hold back anymore and hugged her tight. "I missed you, I missed you a lot. Aditi please can we be like we used to be. I need you. Please"

She neither hugged me back nor respond to what I said.

"Aditya, please it's too late now, I have moved on."

She turned back and was about to close the door.

"Ok so say this to my face. Why can't you face me now?"

"Aditya I can face you. Don't think I don't have the guts to face you. I have moved on now and you should too"

"Wow! Aditi Sharma has moved on" I said sarcastically, "She has moved back to her boring lonely life. Am I right Aditi?"

She remained silent.

"She has chosen a life in which there is no one to share anything with her. She is all alone"

"At least when that way people like you can't hurt me"

"Aditi don't forget that you also hurt me. You had forgiven me for what I had done, and you still left me without any apparent reason.. There is something else that was bothering you. I have been breaking my head over this for months now"

She shouted at the top of her voice, "Stop this discussion Aditya. This all is too painful for me"

"You think that this is not painful for me. Did you ever think how painful it will be for me when one fine day you will just decide and walk away from my life. Did you even think for a moment how it would make me feel? You called me selfish, but you are no different. You had no right to play with my emotions and my life like this"

"It's not like that, I had no other option"

"You always had an option to talk to me. To share what was bothering you. You had an option to tell me the reason why were you leaving me. And well, you still have that option"

I said this hoping she might open up.

"I have moved on Aditya, I have nothing to tell you."

"Aditi, why have you become so difficult? Are you happy seeing me like this, frustrated?"

She remained silent.

"So now you go silent on me, I am really fed up of all this. I am just so tired of this game you are playing. I am leaving for

America tomorrow. I thought before starting a new journey I should try one last time to patch up with you. Nandini Di always sided with you, always asked me not to lose hope and try to talk to you. Finally, even she got tired and asked me to focus on my future. I was a fool to come here. So, I am going to leave now, and this time, I won't turn back. I really won't"

She was shocked and she broke into tears. I left her like that, still unable to comprehend anything. I walked towards my bike.

She ran towards me and hugged me.

"Aditi, sorry but it is too late now" I removed her hands away and continued waking.

"Aditya, not everything is in our hands, some stories just remain incomplete because of that. We have to let go of some things not because we want to, but because we need to"

"Aditi, we are the masters of our destiny. Nothing happens on its own"

I started my bike and left. It was impossible to comprehend anything and I had given up all hope.

Would I ever get to know why did she leave me? I asked myself, and I had no answer.

26

New stories

I woke up at 4 that morning, I had a flight to catch at 6. I had to be at the airport by 5 so I could move ahead with security check in of my luggage and go through my papers once again.

Mom and Raghu uncle had come to see me off at the airport. Raghu uncle had never gotten married, he said he never found the right person. Now mom was going to stay with him while I would be in the US pursuing my degree.

"Adi, call me every day, ok? And don't eat outside food, go with what you get in your dorm. Focus on your studies and make me proud", mom said as she hugged me.

"Sure mom, I will. And you can call me whenever you want to. I will make you proud, I promise. You please take care, I will miss you a lot"

"I will miss you too. Call me as soon as you reach."

"Yup."

With that I waved them good bye and walked into the departure terminal. The time had come leave all the old stories behind and to write new ones. I was overwhelmed at the thought of beginning this new life.

I reached Cambridge more than 24 hours later at about 9:45 AM. I cleared the immigrations and visa checks, and as I stepped out of the airport, all I saw around me was huge, tall buildings. The city was amazingly beautiful, and yet I missed the narrow lanes and the sights and smells of Vadodara, not to say that I missed mom and too a small extent, I missed Aditi too. I reminded myself that I had closed the 'Aditi' chapter before I left India and I didn't have to think about her anymore.

I called mom.

"Hello mom, I reached Cambridge, just came out of the airport. I will go to the college now. How are you?"

"Hello Adi, how are you? How was your flight?"

"I am good mom. The flight was nice. How are you?"

"Good, good, beta. I am good too"

"Ok mom, let me reach college now, I will call you again after that"

"Ok, call me when you get a chance. Bye. Take care."

"Bye mom."

I hailed a cab and went to the lush 168 acre MIT campus. The hostel and student facilities were located in the western end of the campus while the academic buildings were at the eastern end.

I reported to the Administrative block first to confirm my arrival and complete the formalities, while also taking down what room in the dorm I would be residing in.

"Excuse me sir, I am Mr. Aditya Patel, from India, Mechanical Engineering branch. Here are my papers. Could you please help me with which hostel room I would be allocated?"

As he was checking all the details, I saw a girl coming towards the Administration office. She wore black shorts and a white crop top. She had shoulder length hair and she was carrying a lot of luggage. With her black high heeled shoes, it definitely didn't look like she was doing a good job of handling all her luggage and herself. As luck would have it, she lost balance and slipped on the floor, I immediately ran to help her. I offered her my hand for support, and stood back up with its support. I helped her pick up her luggage.

"Thanks"

"The pleasure is mine. On your way to the Admin office?"

"Yes"

"I am going there too, let me give you a hand here"

"Thanks!"

I smiled. "So, are you from India?"

"Yup, from Delhi. And you?"

"I am from India too, from Vadodara, in Gujarat"

"Actually, anyways it doesn't matter where you were is your past, where you are now is what matters"

"Quite a deep thought, I must say"

"Mmmmm… I didn't quite catch your name.."

"Aditya, Aditya Patel."

"I am Avantika Shekhawat." With that, we shook hands.

"So which branch are you in?" I asked her.

"Mechanical engineering"

"Woa! I am in Mechanical too!!"

"Well, nice to meet you"

We reached the admin office.

The officer there told us, "Sorry, but you cannot get your hostel rooms from today. Your academic year begins tomorrow, so the rooms will also get allocated tomorrow"

"Please sir, would there be any way at all you could help us? I don't know anyone here"

"I understand, but I am sorry, this is the Institution's policy"

I was at a loss of ideas now. I could not afford a hotel for the night. I just didn't know what to do.

"Oh god! What will I do now!"

"You can check into a hotel for the night?", she said simply.

"That would strain my budget, I am here on a scholarship"

"You must be super intelligent then. I am a good student myself, but not extraordinary to get a scholarship here"

"That's fine, but I am stuck here, I have no idea what to do now!"

"If you want, and if It's ok with you, you can stay at my place? My father helped me buy an apartment here."

I was frankly a bit taken aback. I had just met her and she was asking me if I was ok with spending the night at her place.

"Don't get shocked, I am just returning the favor! You helped me with the luggage, I am helping you with accommodation for the night"

I thought for a while.

"Do you have any other ideas?"

In a way, she was right; I had no options here that would suit my budget. I reluctantly agreed to camp at her place for the night.

"Ok then, let's go. Please let me know if there is something I could do for you."

"I am having a really bad jet lag, the flight as quite tiring. I would like to rest for a while. Let's go"

I picked up all of mine and half of her luggage. Put me into a red shirt and white trousers and I would look just like those coolies one would find on the railway station back home.

"My apartment is nearby. We can walk. We won't need a cab"

I gave her a strange look.

"I didn't speak Latin, I am sure. Why are you glaring at me? Did I say something wrong?"

"You are weird"

"What makes you say that?"

"You can get a whole apartment in Cambridge, but you wouldn't want to spend on a cab. That's strange"

"My apartment is just two minutes away. Just because I have a lot of money, doesn't mean I should just spend it all around. It wouldn't harm to save some when I can"

"You wear a Dior dress, carry a Louis Vitton bag and talk of saving money. You are full of surprises!"

"You are quite a keen observer!"

We reached her apartment. It was a very comfortable and cozy apartment. The apartment cost around $295,00; that's more than one crore rupees in the Indian currency. It was a simple

1BHK. The bedroom had a nice balcony with an amazing view outside.

"Are you hungry?"

I was more tired than I was hungry. I was wondering what kind of food she could cook.

"Don't worry I am not going to cook! I am ordering from the restaurant."

"Umm…" I was deciding by how many dollars would I be set behind before the next morning, when she said "I will pay, you needn't worry"

"Well then, I am very hungry. Order whatever you like! Free treats are always welcome!"

We laughed. She ordered the food while I went in to freshen up and remove some traces of the long flight.

27

Pristine Friendship

The apartment was well furnished and ready-to-use. The bathroom was also spacious and well equipped.

I took a hot shower. Baroda was always so hot that I never needed a hot shower there. But here it was totally opposite. Summers in Cambridge were cool and pleasant, winters would definitely be colder.

The hot shower refreshed and relaxed me. All my fatigue got washed off and I could feel the energy coming back into me. I wrapped my towel around my waist and came out.

There was a large cupboard right opposite the bathroom, and Avantika was arranging her clothes in it. She was just about to turn back, when I shouted, "Avantika stop! Please don't turn around"

"What happened?"

"There is just a little technical problem…"

"Aditya please I am really tired, I am in no mood for any games? I am turning around now, I need to get my stuff"

"No, no don't turn. I forgot my clothes outside and I stepped out of the shower in just a towel…"

"You have a towel around you, right?"

"Yes"

"Then what's the problem?"

"No, no stop. Please don't turn around"

"So what do you want me to do?"

"Close your eyes and cover them with your fingers"

"Oh come on Aditya, I am already facing away from you! I can't see you!"

"Just do what I say, please." She started laughing. .

"Ok fine, Mr. Shy."

I quickly put on a yellow Donald Duck shirt and track pants. I loved them. There was nothing more comfortable than this.

"Are you done now?"

"Yes, I am done. You can open your eyes and turn in whatever direction you want"

"Finally!"

I was walking out of the room when she stopped me and said, "You are too cute, you know"

She pulled my cheeks, I smiled.

The lunch arrived from the restaurant. We cleaned it all up in no time, and decided to rest after that. I slept on the couch in the living room, while she slept in the bedroom. We would have the same arrangement in the night.

We woke up in the evening and walked over to the river Charles. It was nice and cool with a gentle breeze. I so wished if only Aditi could be with her right now. I missed her a lot. Instead I was killing time and going on long walks with Avantika. Avantika seemed like a nice person, but she couldn't replace Aditi in my mind. Avantika could make me laugh with her jokes, she shared details of her life in Delhi, I quietly listened.

"Now I realize why everybody wants to come and live in America! It is so beautiful and grand!" she was looking at the river as she said that"

"Yup, but nobody thinks of making India like this so nobody would want to immigrate then"

"That would never be possible. India is way too diverse and the government has no control. India can never be what America is"

"we deserve our government, we ourselves are responsible for the mess we make"

"You have a point. But why are we talking about this. It is such a lovely weather, and we are talking governments and social responsibilities! Can we continue this discussion some other day please?"

"Hmmm"

"Tell me about yourself, Aditya; how was your life in Vadodara?"

"It was simple and nice".

"Ummm.. well I meant your love life… Any girlfriends waiting for your return?"

"My studies have been my only focus, I had no time for girlfriends"

"I don't buy that!"

"Why? How can you be so sure?"

"Dude, just look at you. You are perfect. Every girl's mother would like a son – in – law like you. And every girl would desire someone like you. You look great, you are intelligent and smart, and you are so kind and genuine. What else do girls want? I am sure any girl would fall for you."

I did not want any girl I just wanted Aditi.

"Well thanks, I will take that as a compliment"

"It was undoubtedly meant as one. Whoever you fall for, would be a really lucky woman, I am sure"

I got lost in Aditi's thoughts. What would she be doing right now? Would she be fine? It was too painful for me to leave her like that, I didn't even know what she felt about me going off to MIT. But she had left me with no other option!

"Hey! Hello! Are you there?"

"Yeah, I was thinking where to go next"

"Don't lie Aditya, you are a pathetic liar! You were thinking about someone"

"No, I don't have nobody to think of"

"There was someone special in your life, wasn't there?"

This was getting a little uncomfortable now, "No Avantika, can we please talk something else?"

"Oh I am glad you almost accepted it! There was someone special in your life. It's ok if you don't want to talk about it. You can ask me anything you want, I have no secrets. I just say whatever is there in my mind, and don't keep piling up things inside my head"

"You are right, but sometimes some things just get left incomplete. Completing them becomes more painful, and it is just better to leave it as it is. Talking about it doesn't do any good either"

"Wow, you are such a philo! My turn to talk serious stuff now!"

"Sure, go ahead!"

28

Knowing each other

"I have officially had 24 boyfriends till now. I broke up with the 25th one before I flew here"

"Cool! Were any of these relationships serious or were they just casual flings..."

"they were all pretty casual, sometimes just for fun and entertainment, sometimes just to have some company and have someone pay my bills!, she said naughtily.

"This is what I hate about you girls. You pretend you love us like there is no tomorrow, but actually you just use the men. Like for what, entertainment? Please go home and switch on the TV man!. You say you are in love and then few days later you would dump us for no reason. You realize how inhuman that is? I seriously pity the 25 boys who wasted their time on a girl like you"

It was my anger on Aditi that was coming out on Avantika.

"Hey you are being judgmental. Just because I had 25 boyfriends does not mean I don't have a heart. It's just that I couldn't find the right guy"

"Oh, you will always find a reason to escape. I am beginning to pity myself or spending time with you"

I had hurt her for no fault of hers. I was venting out my anger on her, and that was wrong. It took me a moment too long to realize my mistake. I calmed myself but I had no idea how to cover up for it.

"Nobody has ever talked to me like this. Nobody asked you to spend time with me. You want to leave, go, walk free. I am not holding you down here"

"Avantika, I am really sorry. Please calm down… I should not have talked to you like this. I got a little carried away and vented somebody else's anger on you"

"I get that! But you don't get to talk to me like this. Like how dare you talk to me like that? How dare you judge me for anything?"

"I am really sorry Avantika, I didn't mean any of what I said, I really got carried away. My life has turned topsy-turvy in the past some time and it has been quite frustrating. I thought maybe a change of place would help me put my past behind me, but it is not going out of head, not for now at least. And it is driving me crazy. I really apologize for the outburst"

"You got dumped or something?"

"Not quite, it is slightly more complicated than that"

"You wanna talk about it?"

I did not reply. I did not want to remember all the incidents again. I wanted to forget them. The more I talked about it, the more the memories remained fresh in my head.

"Ok, fine, but at least cheer up. You can't change what has already happened. Just try and engage yourself in something else"

"Yup, I will try my best."

We visited the MIT Chapel then and spent some time in the Jack Barry Astro Turf Field within the MIT Avenue. We also visited the MIT museum. It was fun exploring the city on foot. On our way, Avantika stopped at a wine shop and bought a bottle of wine while I waited outside for her. She didn't know I did not drink alcohol, I didn't mention it to her either. I thought I might as well wait for her to bring it up.

After visiting the MIT Museum, we saw Toscanini's Ice Cream shop on our way. Avantika decided to have some ice cream, so we went into Toscanini's. She ordered butterscotch, I ordered chocolate. That night we had dinner at McDonald's. It was a stone throw's away from Toscanini's. MIT is surrounded by great restaurants like Bertucci's, CuchiCuchi, Beijing Tokyo, Royal East, Salts and Cargie On Main, but all these names were totally new for us. We had had a long day, and we weren't in a mood to experiment anything much, McDonald's that way was a safe bet. It took us a little more time and some more walking before we could reach McDonald's but it was worth it.

We were really exhausted by the time we finished dinner, we had no more energy to walk anymore. We decided to take a cab. A thought hit me that maybe had Aditi been here, she would still have preferred to walk back, she never ever got tired. I realized that I wasn't even vaguely over her, for everything I did, I would automatically think what Aditi would have done, or what she would have said. She would just not go out of my mind.

Once we reached home, I worked on making the couch comfortable enough to spend the night on it while Avantika changed into her blue Sponge Bob Square pants pajamas.

She came out of her room and asked, "Why are you off to bed so early?"

"Doesn't everyone sleep at night? The last I checked, I wasn't a nocturnal animal"

"Dude it's just 10!. Who sleeps so early?"

"It's not too early for me. And I am really tired"

"Oh come on. I will be alone here from tomorrow. I won't have anybody to have fun with! Come on, for my sake!", she made a puppy face as she said that.

"Alright, what do you wanna do?"

She took out the bottle of wine. "This is the plan"

I hesitated, I did not know what to answer. But sometimes, silence is the best answer.

"Don't tell me you don't drink"

"I don't. Gujarat is a dry state, I have never even tried any alcohol, nor do I want to"

"Give it a shot, I am sure you will like it. You have no idea what you are missing"

"No Avantika, please don't. I don't want to. We have a beautiful life, I wouldn't want to ruin it for a temporary celebration or a show off with alcohol"

"Woa! That was deep. Well, if you won't drink, I won't either. But for the record, alcohol doesn't really ruin lives"

She went on into the kitchen. I realized this was more of Aditi thinking, than my own thoughts. Aditi would always look at the bigger picture, she would always think of the future.

Avantika came out with two glasses of water.

"Sorry I do not have anything else to drink."

"That's ok, I was thirsty anyways"

"Cheers to our new friendship."

"Cheers"

"So were you in love or something?", she said after a while.

"I was but my story got left incomplete and I doubt it will ever complete"

"Have faith Aditya. Destiny will carve a path for itself, and maybe your paths will cross again"

"I have given up all hope Avantika, I don't think that's possible"

"No Aditya, come on, don't lose hope"

"I don't really believe in love anymore"

"She must have been really close. Who was she?"

"Aditi Sharma. She was a cute little angel who changed my life. "Aditi Sharma. She was a cute little angel who changed my life. She was so beautiful, she was refreshing like petrichor."

"Thats a new word. What's petrichor?"

"Its the fragrance of wet mud from the first rains."

"oh. So what went wrong?"

"Well, the monsoon ended, and the fragrance went away!"

"Very funny. Why did she leave you?"

"I have absolutely no idea"

"So will you be able to forgive and forget her?"

"People say time heals every wound. Let's see if that really happens"

29

Self realizations

I woke up early the next morning, it was the first day of college and I was super excited. How many years had I spent dreaming of this day! For a person like me habituated to waking up at 9, waking up at 5:30 was way too early. I went into the kitchen and decided to make some coffee for Avantika and me.

Avantika seemed to belong to a really very affluent family, she was bold and carefree. She put up a show that she could flirt with anyone and avoid commitments, but she seemed really innocent and sweet at heart.

I was going to spend the next four years here, and it was good to have made a good friend on my first day itself.

I searched through the entire refrigerator. There was no milk, no sugar, no coffee. I had no idea if there would even be a shop open at this ungodly hour. With nothing better to do, I decided to call mom. It must be around 3PM for her

"Hello Mom"

"Adi, how are you? I was waiting for your call. Did you sleep well? How is your hostel room? How is the college campus?"

"It's fabulous mom. I have never seen something so marvelous like this. The campus is really magnificent. I am really excited to study here"

That's nice. And what about the room, how is it?"

"Mom actually there was a small problem"

"What happened Adi, is everything alright?"

I could sense mom getting a bit hyper.

"Mom, relax there is nothing to worry. The college authorities refused to give out the rooms yesterday as the academic year begins only today. I couldn't afford a hotel here. I then met someone in the corridor and we became friends. That friend's dad is super rich and he has bought an apartment near the college. So I spent the night there"

"Is your friend a girl or a boy?"

It would have been a very, very bad idea to tell mom that on my first day out of India, in Cambridge, I had spent the entire night at a girl's house. She would put me on the next plane back home then for sure!

"Mom, how can it be a girl? Of course it's a guy!"

"Good. Reach college early today and get your room"

"Sure mom. I should go now, the bill is piling up. Will call you later. Bye. Take care"

"Bye"

I wanted to call Nandini Di too but decided to do so in the evening. With making coffee not an option, I decided to take a shower and get dressed. I chose a simple blue t-shirt and black jeans. Aditi used to love my simplicity. After the shower, I packed my bags and set my hair.

It was almost 7, at least some shop should have opened by now. Avantika was still fast asleep. I didn't want to disturb her, I tiptoed around and pulled the curtains. I remembered the days when I would never wake up before 9. The only time I woke up early was when I had to go to school. Aditi had played a big role in changing those habits. In fact, thanks to Aditi, I hadn't slept at all in the past few months. Considering that, I had a very, very peaceful sleep last night.

I went into the living room, took the keys and locked the apartment. This was a good call, I guess. The weather outside was superb. The cool breeze was tantalizing, everything around was pristine.

A moment ago, I had been reeling under the weight of my past, and now I felt like a stranger. Nature often has its own ways to make you see the beauty of your own life. The leaves and branches swaying in the breeze tell you that just go with the flow, don't resist it, don't try to comprehend everything. The cool breeze tells you to be free. I told myself that if destiny wanted, Aditi would come back someday, that I needed to let her go for now.

I was surprised to see that all the shops were open. The college was about to start in sometime. I walked around and found a Citibank ATM. I withdrew some cash and continued my walk. I found a lot of shops in my way like H mart, Big Apple, Rulls, etc. I was the happiest when I saw Shalimar India Food and Spices, and decided to buy the milk and coffee from here. It was like a complete normal Indian grocery store with all the vegetables, pickles and spices. I bought everything that I thought Avantika might find useful and some more things that I needed. Then I began walking back to Avantika's apartment with my hands full of grocery bags.

30

MIT here I come!

It was a task to open the lock when I reached Avantika's place, with all the bags in my hand, but I managed somehow. I went straight to the kitchen and put the bags down. I went on to Avantika's room to check if she had woken up. She had not. She was sleeping like a baby. I had to wake her up or she would be late for college. I went in and and sat by her bed, but I didn't know how to wake her up. Should I touch her, should I call her name. I chose the latter. "Avantika, Avantika wake up!" This didn't seem to be working. I was about to hold her by her shoulder and shake her up, when she opened her eyes. she was a little shocked seeing me so close so she got up in a swift

"Avantika, calm down! I was trying to wake you up. It is 8 o'clock already and it is our first day of college!"

It took a moment for reality to hit her, "Oh man! You seriously freaked me out!"

"I am sorry, I didn't intend to"

"Cool. So I need to take a shower and get dressed quickly, and then I will be ready. I see you are already set here. Wait a few minutes, I will join you, then we can leave"

"No Avantika, I need to go early, as I have to get my dorm. You can come at the regular time"

"I thought could both go together and get your dorm"

"Well, ok. That should be good too. Waiting alone in the admin office is not a great idea, I could use some company"

Her face lit up, "I will be ready and meet you outside in five"

I knew women better than that to know that women never get ready in five, even when they say so with full conviction.

I went to the kitchen to make some coffee. I kept it a little light and poured the coffee into two cups and took them to Avantika's room. To my surprise, when I knocked on her door, she was all dressed and ready. She wore light blue jeans, and a dark blue crop top. Her hair was messy and it looked cool on her. She opened her cupboard to take out some other accessories to go with her look. Her wardrobe was full of shorts, miniskirts, short dresses, jeans, and lots of crop tops. All the clothes were branded and looked pretty expensive. And there were a lot of accessories. She had handbags of every single brand you could imagine - Chanel, Fendi; Hermes, Prada, Louis Vuitton, etc, she had it all She took out a very beautiful bracelet. She turned towards the door to go out in the living room, and saw me there, holding out a mug of coffee. "Coffee for you"

I handed the mug over to her. "Thank you so much! This is just what I needed!"

"Can we have coffee in the balcony, I would always do that back in India, it is a great experience to have"

"Meeting you was the best experience in itself" she mumbled it below her breath, but I still managed to hear it..

I pretended ignorance, "Sorry did you say something?"

"Nope nothing at all, let's go to the balcony"

I did not push it any further and I didn't think much about it.

We went to the balcony. It was great to have a hot coffee in the cool weather.

"I would have my coffee in the balcony every morning back home, I so loved it. But I could do that only on the days I woke up early"

"I thought you were an early riser"

"No, earlier I would never get up before nine. But things change"

Aditi came running back into my head, and I took a deep breath and pushed her out

"Do you know Aditya, life is so long. We meet so many people. Some stay, some go away. Some might go away and still live in our hearts"

"Some people just vanish off without a warning"

"Even if they vanish they remain in our memories. Unlike computers, life doesn't have an option to delete unwanted files"

"Life would be so much simpler if we could erase memories we don't want to keep anymore"

"Give it some time. Memories fade away with time. New memories overwrite the past ones"

"Yes, you are right. Time to go to college!"

"Yup let's go. I am sure it will be a great day today."

We walked college. I had butterflies inside me, I was so excited and nervous. We reached Admin office in a few minutes.

"Good morning sir. I am Aditya Patel. I had come yesterday as well regarding my hostel room. I just wanted to check if I could get it now?"

"One minute let me check."

He typed my name in his computer and checked my details.

"Yes Aditya Patel, from India. You are on a full scholarship, correct?"

"Yes, sir"

"Here, take your room keys. Two people are going to share one room. You room partner is Alex Wrington. He must be on his way I guess. Till then you can make yourself comfortable"

"Thanks a lot sir"

"You are welcome. Have a nice day young man"

Avantika and I left the admin office. She accompanied me to the hostel gate.

"I am hungry. I will go and take a round of the campus and search some place to have our breakfast. Till then you get settled in your room"

"Cool. Text me as soon as you find something"

We parted ways. The admin office was quite some distance from the MIT main office. The hostel blocks, subway, MIT Co-op was in the opposite direction. So we had to walk a lot. I finally found my room - room number was 203. There was nothing grand about the room, but it was by no means ordinary either. I could smell the new bed sheets as I opened the door. There were two beds to my right, with a table in between and the two study tables on the left. The washroom was in the opposite corner. There was a huge window right opposite the door. I walked across the room and opened the window to let some fresh air in. I had just put down all my luggage when Avantika's text arrived, asking me to Dunkin Donuts, near MIT Co-op. It was quite some distance from my dorm. I wanted to wait for my new roommate, but I didn't want to keep Avantika waiting either. I pushed my luggage below the bed, locked the room and went to Dunkin Donuts.

MIT was a world in itself. Each and every facility was available here. There were innumerable libraries, eateries, huge auditoriums, advanced and well equipped laboratories and lots more. There were enormous gardens where we could sit and study or just jam away. One could never tire away in the campus.

31

Friendly first day

I reached Dunkin's and as I pushed the door open, I could catch the aroma of fresh donuts and coffee. I looked for Avantik inside, she was at the table in the corner. I walked across the café and took the seat next to her.

"That was pretty quick."

"Well I am hungry too"

She was still undecided over what she wanted to have, but we went and stood up in the short queue. She took a Butternut donut and a cappuccino. I was a lot more hungry than she was, so I ordered Chocolate coconut cake donut and Egg and cheese sandwich. They didn't seem to have any other vegetarian sandwich available at the moment.

We went back to our table and sat in silence, we were out of things to talk about. Now this was getting really awkward.

"So besides making boyfriends, what are your other hobbies?" I said breaking the silence.

"I like to swim. I have been a state level champion in swimming. But swimming leads to a lot of tough tanning, so I quit!"

That was a really strange reason to quit, but I didn't say anything. Our order had just arrived.

"So you were not really passionate about it, were you?"

"There isn't anything much in my life that I am really passionate about"

"Well, the way I look at it, having a passion in life makes life worth living, you have something to live for then!"

"Not everybody is a brainy nerd like you!"

"you don't need to be a brainy nerd to be passionate about something. You just need to dedicate yourself to something. Like you can focus on your studies now, you are at the grandest and one of the most coveted colleges of the world. Students work really hard to secure an admission here, some of them who manage to get an admission here sometimes don't get a scholarship and are not able to make it then. You are lucky to be a student here"

"I know how lucky I am. You don't have to explain it to me", she sounded agitated and rude.

"Alright, chill man. Are you at least interested in pursuing engineering as a career?"

"Nope, I have no interest in engineering at all"

"Then what are you doing here? You might as well have told your dad about it, you could have saved him a lot of money and trouble"

"We have classes to attend, time to leave!"

She cut me short and walked off. She seemed to have gone a bit pale. I felt guilty that I had spoilt her mood on the very first day of the college. Maybe it was not a very good idea to rain a motivation speech on her.

I quickly followed her, I ran to catch up with her and blocked her path. She was crying. I could not believe my eyes. She was actually crying! She wiped off her tears and looking down.

"Avantika are you alright?"

"Yes, I am fine. We have a long distance to cover, let's walk fast, we don't want to be late on the very first day of college"

She tried sounding normal but quite evidently she didn't feel that way.

"Avantika, look I am sorry. I didn't mean to offend you. I am the 'plan and act' kinda guy; I rarely do anything without planning. I just find it a little hard to digest that one can even go on with life without an aim. Please don't get me wrong"

"Cool. No offence taken. So chill and keep walking"

"Then why are you crying?"

She chose to keep quiet. That was my cue to back off and not probe any further.

"Oh forget it. Let's go to the class. We are seriously getting late."

We reached the class in a while. The class was almost full. There were five rows of circular desks for the students, with fifteen students occupying each row. The students were arranged alphabetically across the class and each seat held a student's name who would occupy that seat. My name, beginning with 'A', got the second desk, right in the beginning itself, and my neighbor on the first desk was someone called Addison. I had Alex on the third seat, my neighbor to the right. And Avantika was on seat number 4. It felt good to have Avantika close by. Avantika settled in her chair and smiled at me. I smiled back and settled into my seat.

Alex came in a few minutes later and asked me, "You are Aditya Patel, right?"

He had a funny way of pronouncing my last name but I chose to ignore it. "Yes I am Aditya. Hi Alex!"

"Hey bro! How have you been? The officer in the Admin Office mentioned that I am sharing my dorm with you"

"I am doing great, thank you. Glad to have you as a roommate"

"So, are you from India?"

"Yes, you guessed it right. How about you, are you a local here?"

"Nope I have come from Houston, Texas"

"Nice, it is really nice to meet you"

"Why are you being so formal?"

He stood up and did his peculiar handshake with me.

"Now we are buddies man!"

"Great!"

"It's gonna be fun studying here. You cannot even imagine how much we are going to enjoy"

"Yes, I definitely hope so"

He came closer and whispered, "Man, who this pretty girl sitting next to me? She is really hot dude!"

I guess this is how men are, irrespective of where they come from. I unlike most men, had never thought of women like that.

I looked at Avantika, I had no idea how to answer Alex's question. She looked up and saw me staring at her. "What?"

"Nothing"

I turned back to Alex and said, "She is Avantika. She is also from India"

"Cool. Desi girls are not too bad! Do you happen to know her?"

"I met her this morning. Since we are both from India, we caught on quickly"

"Great dude, You are fast!"

I wasn't in a mood to tell Alex that I had spent the last night at Avantika's place. I was saved when our Mathematics Professor, Prof Joseph entered the class. He was dressed in a suit, must have been fifity-ish and gave a casual introduction speech.

We had back-to back lectures for the rest of the day. First day of class in school used to be fun, first day at MIT was full of lectures and assignments.

Thinking of the first day of class reminded me of Aditi, I evidently could not get over her. I still believed she loved me, but I didn't know why she had pushed me away. I missed her a lot.

32

All happy. Am I?

We had a break for the next hour and a half, Avantika and I walked out of the class together and decided to go to Subway for lunch. It was good to have such long breaks, consider we had to walk such long distances. I realized I should have invited Alex to join us, not because he called Avantika hot, but because he was my roomie. I turned to look around and saw him walking all alone.

"Avantika, just wait for a sec"

I ran over to Alex, "Hey Alex, Avantika and I are going to subway to grab some lunch. Do you want to come along?"

"Is Avantika also going to be there? Then I will join you", we ran back together to where Avantika was waiting.

"So Alex, this is Avantika; Avantika, this is Alex"

I thought they needed an introduction but I couldn't be more mistaken.

"Avantika is such a gorgeous name. It's just as beautiful as you are"

"Thanks! Well, I must say you are quite appealing yourself! And you also have an interesting name!"

"Obviously an interesting person has to go by an interesting name! If I may say so, Subway is a boring idea. There is a really nice café just around the corner. If you guys are ok with it, we should go there for lunch"

"Sure, why not!", Avantika was quick to reply

Alex took a step back and requested me to go to Subway in a whispering voice, he wanted to be alone with Avantika. I decided to oblige, "You guys carry on, I would rather stick with my sub"

I smiled back at the two of them. I felt Avantika was sure to get bored in my company. And then Alex seemed to really like her. So Avantika had maybe found someone whose company she could enjoy.

I went on to Subway and ordered a veggie patty. Gobbled it all up and started on my way back to class as fast as I could. When I reached class, I saw Avantika and Alex had not returned yet.

I decided to flip through the books for the next lecture. A while later they entered the class holding hands.

"Dude, do I see you studying on the first day here?"

"Not really, I was just flipping through the books for the next class we have"

At the end of Day 1 at MIT, I had two new friends – Avantika and Alex. They both seemed to get each other better than I got either one of them.

That night after we had turned the lights off and were about to hit the sack I asked Alex what he thought about Avantika,

"She is hot and really interesting. We are really going to have fun!"

"I meant, if you had some love at first sight kinda thing with her?"

"Dude, hold on, you are on some different trajectory and have taken things too far. There is nothing like love or anything between us. We are just two young individuals who are attracted to each other. We will spend some time together, have fun; and then eventually we will get tired of each other. We definitely won't last together beyond a year!"

"Oh, oh, ok!"

The theory of changing girlfriends every month was out of my syllabus so it was completely beyond me. It was difficult for me to get over one girl in my life and I was struggling to comprehend how Alex managed to get over someone every month, every year?

It had been five months at MIT. Avantika, Alex and I had became the closest buddies and would always be found together. We would take selfies almost every day – crazy ones, serious ones, everything. I would feel a bit lonely, when Avantika and Alex would have their lovey-dovey time together, but Avantika would make sure that I didn't feel left out and they both spent equal time with me too.

At home also everything was going good. Mom was doing better. Nandini Di was also happy and settled in her life.

Everyone around me was happy and satisfied with their lives, except me. I had not got over Aditi. I just couldn't push her out of my head, I didn't think I would ever be able to do it. But I kept my feelings to myself, I never showed it to anyone. Life went on at MIT and I put on a happy face and continued with my dream.

"Aditya can you please help me with this, I just can't get this into my head", Avantika asked me. Alex and I had come over to her apartment to study. We were preparing for the mid-term examinations coming up next month.

"Ask Alex, he will help you. I am into another chapter right now" I ignored her. Studying with someone reminded me too much of Aditi. Avantika took it up with Alex and got her problem sorted.

Avantika and Alex took a break. Alex went out to get something to eat. Avantika came and sat next to me.

"Come on Aditya take a break with us. Not studying for five minutes won't kill you. We haven't talked to each other about anything but studies for quite some time now"

"Avantika please don't disturb. I have to call mom over dinner, and that would be a really long break for me. That should be enough"

"Aditya please, spend some time with us, we are your friends after all"

"I am spending my entire days with you, what more do you want?"

"Aditya you are there but you are still never really there. You are always lost in your own world"

"Oh come on, you know it's nothing like that" I denied what I knew was a fact.

"Then why do you remain so quiet when we are together? You have just stopped smiling, man. You need to enjoy life more, you live only once. You know you can talk to me if something is bothering you".

"You and Alex are lost in your own dream world all the time, when do you think I should talk to you"

She took my hand in hers and said, "Aditya fix this in your head once and for all, I won't say this again. Alex is temporary but you are permanent. Alex and I will separate in a few months but I want you to stay. I want you to support me, push me, motivate me to be passionate about life! I want to keep smiling over your silly blunders. I value your friendship above everything else"

"I must say you are expecting way too much. Relationships, even friendships have not been my forte"

"Don't worry I trust you. And I know you would learn from your mistakes and won't repeat them" I smiled at her. "Hold on, you look cute when you smile. Just fix this smile forever on your face. You smile like that and you can make any woman go crazy for you"

"Does that include you?" I was hoping for an interesting answer, it was just a tease.

"Didn't you realize that I was already crazy for you? I don't just be friends with anyone!"

I clutched her hand tighter and kept the other hand around her shoulder. I was happy Avantika was the first person to notice that there was something bothering me. It was a relief to know that there was at least somebody who cared enough to understand things I hadn't said.

Alex came in with the food "Hey guys look what I have here" He was about to take something out from his bag when he saw us together holding hands "Oh sorry wrong timing I guess!"

"Oh shut up Alex! Come on in." Avantika stood up and walked towards him. She kissed him on his cheek.

"So what was happening right now?"

"see, you getting all possessive! Nothing was happening, Aditya was a little worried about the exams so I was talking to him and calming him down"

"Why are you so worried? Chill man, you are brilliant, you will clear these exams easily"

"Of course! And I have such great friends, there is no scope to fail!"

"Finally someone realized it"

"Time for a group hug buddies!" Alex said opening his arms. He loved group hugs. We both jumped on him and hugged each other. We ate the food he had got us and wrapped up for the day.

33

Slave of schedules

That night after dinner, I stood by the window in my room and called mom, "Hello Mom..."

"Hello Adi, how are you? How are you studies going on? How is your roommate Alex?"

"Relax mom, breath. I am doing great. Alex, as always, is also great. My studies are going awesome. Alex and I study together and help each other out"

"That's very nice. And Adi how are the other college students? I mean there is no ragging or anything else is going on in the college, right? Is anybody troubling you"

"No mom, the college is really superb. It is very disciplined. Other students here respect me, they think I am really very bright. They are very kind to me."

"Adi, it would be hard for anyone not to like you or respect you. And you are really bright, don't let anybody tell you otherwise. Don't worry about me, I am fine here"

"Yes mom, my full focus is on my studies right now"

"That's like my good boy."

"Ok mom, time to go. I will talk to you later. Bye. Take care"

"Bye dear" It always felt good to talk to mom.

It had been months since I had seen or talked to Aditi, I should have gotten over her by now. But the problem is I hadn't and I didn't know what to do about it, or how to go about it.

I woke up early the next morning to study, while Alex woke up as usual. We got dressed and went off to college. To our surprise Avantika was already waiting for us at Dunkin Donuts. It had become a daily ritual to meet up there before we made our way to our classes. She looked cute in the pink colored short dress she was wearing. Her short hair made her look like a Barbie Doll.

The professor entered the class just as we were settling into our seats. I was engrossed in the lecture. Alex leaned forward on the desk while Avantika leaned back onto the chair. I turned towards her and caught her staring at me. She turned away the moment I caught her gaze.

After classes that day, we went to Zigo Café at one of the extreme corners of the campus. We took a corner table. Avantika and I ended up sitting facing each other with Alex in the middle.

Alex got a call from home, "Hello mom, how are you? How is dad?" He couldn't hear what his mom was saying so he asked her to hold a minute as he got up to walk out of the café. On his way out, he told us, "Guys I will be back soon"

"Sure, take your time, we will be right here"

Avantika stood up from her place and took the seat Alex had just vacated. I was holding the menu with one hand, while my other hand just lay on the table. She quietly brought her soft hand over mine and took my hand in hers. I ignored it and pulled my hand away. She was taken aback, perhaps I was the first guy to reject her and push her back. None of us said anything.

"Let's order" I said breaking the silence. We both ordered a hot cappuccino, it was getting really cold outside.

"Aditya, do you believe in giving second chances to people in your life?"

"Well not really. I mean once the person has cheated you, broken the trust you had in them, no matter how hard you try, the wounds never really heal"

"But isn't time supposed to be the best healer?"

"Maybe. I have never thought that way. Eevrything I had ever believed in had been proved wrong by someone a long time ago; I stopped having any beliefs after that."

"Don't worry and don't lose hope. That's the only belief I have and nobody has ever proved it wrong!"

"But you can't have hopes out of someone who has completely disappeared and given up on you?

"Then keep hope on the people around you. Trust me they won't disappoint you."

She stood up and walked out of the café. I am not sure what she really meant by the last sentence or who the sentence really was for. I did not ponder much over it, I finished my coffee and went back to my room to catch up on my studies. My plan was to cover as much ground as I could the next day, I didn't want to spend any moment when I was not studying. Engineering was no easy thing, and it had made my schedule really tight as the exams approached, giving me little time to think about anything else. I would go to bed at two in the night and wake up at 6:30 in the morning. I was sleep deprived, but I couldn't complain. I had no time to complain or even realize I was sleep deprived.

Alex was quite the opposite – cool and calm. His schedule continue to remain the same and the approaching examinations didn't tend to bring any change in it. He would sleep peacefully at 11, and wake up late and still manage to revise the entire portion. I was surprised at that. Maybe I was a perfectionist so I took longer to finish things as I would always want them to be perfect. This habit had helped me a lot in life, but sometimes it was a curse. Really.

34

Mind wrecking exams

Preparation leave was declared for the week preceding the mid-term examinations. We also had to turn in our assignments after the exams.

Our exams were supposed to begin on 4/12 and my focus was entirely on them. Aditi's thoughts were still a distraction but when had my day ever been complete without thinking about her.

I had called mom on the eve of my exam. It was morning there. I was a little nervous. But I had confidence that everything was going to be great.

"Adi, how are your studies going on? How is everything there?"

"Yes, mom everything is totally fine. Studies are going on really well"

"Wonderful. Now don't get nervous in exams. Remain calm and write well. Read every question twice. Don't forget to take your calculator, pen and other stuff."

"Mom, I am almost 18 now, I hope you remember? And you know I never forget things" I really never forget things. I was never the kid who forgot the notebook or the pen or the homework.

"Yes dear but I am your mom, I tend to get worried, and it is my job to keep reminding you things. Listen, I am getting late for school. I will talk to you later. Bye and take care"

"Bye mom. You too take care"

Finally the examinations began. We had six exams - the first was Applied Mathematics, then there was a day off, then thermodynamics, followed by strength of materials, production process – 1, computer aided Machine drawing, data base retrieval system, and then finally Machine Shop practice 1. Six examinations stretching over a span of 8 days.

But the eight days passed pretty quickly, we breathed a sigh of relief at completing one milestone, however, the assignments were yet to be turned in. But when you have just crossed a big mountain you can still celebrate over the weekend before you fret over the other mountain that still needed to be conquered.

Close to the McDonald's near the MIT campus was a Middle Eastern restaurant and night club. Alex suggested we should go and celebrate there. I neither imbibed spirits nor did I like dancing to such loud music. Dancing in a DJ party in India was one thing, dancing in a night club in the US was another.

I still put on a black tee and beige trousers and accompanied Avantika and Alex there. Avantika was wearing a black shining short dress Alex as always was under-dressed. I decided to take a safe seat at the bar, while Avantika and Alex went off dancing on the floor. They were dancing the night away and I was getting bored all alone. I was just about to get up and leave when Avantika came by and sat on the stool next to me. She was saying something but I could not hear her over the loud music in the club. She came closer and shouted out.

"This place doesn't suit you"

"I know, I was about to leave"

"Come I will make it suit you." she held my hand and dragged me to the dance floor. She tried stepping closer when dancing and I kept stepping back countering her effort to narrow the distance. And Alex was a spectator to this, he definitely wasn't liking what he was seeing. I tried my best to put as much distance as I could between Avantika and me, but the more I tried to move away the more she tried to come closer. I had no idea what was going on here. I could see Alex getting jealous, I didn't mean any of this to happen. I decided to leave Avantika and Alex to their dancing and go back to my safe place at the bar but Avantika held my hand and stopped me. Alex came over and dragged Avantika to a corner, leaving me alone. They were having a heated argument, and there was no guessing what it could have been about. Men will be men after all! I felt guilty to have caused the argument between my best friends.

Avantika walked out on Alex, came to the bar and asked for Vodka shots. She downed two vodka shots and said, "We broke up, as such I was bored of him now!" She smiled and returned back to the dance floor.

After she had left, Alex came over, "We broke up." He also gulped down two shots of vodka.

"I am sorry man. I never intended any of this to happen"

"Don't be, as such I was bored of her" He also smiled and went back to the dance floor.

They hardly looked like they had had a breakup. Here I was unable to forget Aditi and unable to move on, and here were Avantika and Alex who had moved on in a moment. I found it difficult to digest. They were so totally like each other, maybe that's why they couldn't stick together for long.

Both Alex and Avantika got totally drunk that night. Alex was totally unaware of his surroundings or his state of consciousness, while Avantika was still a little better off. I could not take Alex to the hostel like that, so I decided to take him to Avantika's apartment. I half dragged him, half carried him to Avantikas place and laid him down on Avantika's bed.

All settled, Avantika and I sat down on the couch in the living room.

"So all fine?" I asked her.

"Yeah, totally" And then her blabbering started. It was more of alcohol talking that Avantika herself.

"Aditya, you know what, I never loved Alex. He also never loved me. I don't know if I have experienced true love. No one has ever truly loved me in my life, not even my parents"

"No Avantika it's not like that. Parents always love their children. Their love is unconditional"

"No Aditya, if they loved me they would not have stopped me. They would not have restricted me."

"Avantika, parents restrict us for our benefit. Trust me, I have been there too. Today I so regret not listening to my mom"

"No, it's not like that. I wanted to be a fashion photographer. It was my dream since I was a kid. But when I told this to my parents, they ruined everything in seconds"

"Avantika, it's because they wanted that you get a secured future"

"No Aditya. My elder sister is a Harvard university topper but that does not mean I should also be like her"

"Avantika you should sleep, you must be tired; it's been a long day" This was getting into personal territory and the last thing I wanted was to be meddled in Avantika's family affairs. I had enough of my own to sort through. But you can't stop Avantika, and definitely not a drunk Avantika.

"No Aditya, you cannot change the topic like this"

"See Avantika this is your Family matter. I shouldn't get involved in it"

"Ok fine don't get involved in this. But what about us? How will you ignore it?"

"Avantika what are you talking about? Listen, you are drunk and you should sleep now"

"Oh just shut up! A few drinks hardly bother me. Come on Aditya, don't feign ignorance"

"Avantika I have no idea what you are talking about"

"Oh come on man, wake up, open your eyes. I danced close to you deliberately tonight at the club. How else would I have got a reason to break up with Alex?"

"So?"

"So then I left him"

"So you left him, fine. But what do I have to do with that?"

She got furious and stood up. I also stood up.

"Aditya are you blind. Can't you see? I love you dammit!"

For a moment there was utter silence. I was shocked. More than shocked, I was scared. I did not want to damage my friendship with Avantika.

After a while, she pushed me towards the wall and pinned me there, "I gave you so many signs but you ignored all. I loved you from day one. Today I broke up with Alex just because of you. I love you Aditya, don't you get it?"

She came close to me and was about to kiss me. I closed my eyes and saw Aditi in my mind.

"No Avantika this is wrong." I pushed her away.

"Falling in love is not wrong Aditya"

"No Avantika this cannot happen. I love someone else"

"Oh come on Aditya that girl has already left you. How long are you going to mourn her loss? Move on Aditya, just move on"

."No Avantika I can't. I can't forget her. I will be cheating on her if I get involved with you. And that guilt would kill me. My love for her hasn't died"

"So what about me? What about my love? It will also never die!"

"Avantika can we talk about this later on, it's quite late."

"No Aditya I want to discuss this right now. So answer me. What will happen to me? Have you ever thought of that?"

I did not have any answer for this question.

"You don't, do you? Just leave Aditya. Go to your hostel and sleep. You will never have an answer to my question"

I left Avantika's place and made my way back to my dorm.

Once in my room, I stood by the window looking up at the starry sky. It reminded me of how happy Aditi would feel looking at the stars and the sky. I could see her sparkling eyes and the glow on her face in my mind. All those happy memories from the past came swimming back in my mind. It broke my heart to realize that I couldn't live those moments again. They were only left behind as memories now. Maybe had Aditi still been with me, I wouldn't have lost Avantika as a friend.

Sleep was the last thing that came to me that night. I was worried how I would face Avantika the next morning and how I would handle the situation. I did not want to lose Avantika, she was a really good friend, but I didn't love her either.

35

Unexpected understandings

In the morning, I was sprawled on the floor of my dorm, by the window. The warmth and light of the sun penetrating through the open window woke me up. It was going to be a tough day. We had no classes today, it was Sunday after all. Avantika wouldn't want to see me after what had happened last night. I now had one more day to go over what had happened and curse my life for bringing me to this situation.

I took a hot shower and got dressed. I called Alex to enquire if he was feeling alright after being completely drunk last night. He said he would be in the dorm in five. I was worried about Avantika too, I wanted to ask about her. But decided against it and just hung up.

I began working on an assignment when my phone buzzed upon receiving a text. It was from Avantika I didn't want to lose her, I didn't know what to talk to her about.

"Come to the Martin Luther King Jr. Garden in five minutes. I am waiting there for you"

The garden was near MIT FCU and MIT Co-op. I jogged my way to the garden. She was sitting on a bench opposite the entrance to the garden. I went up to her and sat next to her.

"See Avantika, let's just forget whatever happened last night. Let's call it a nightmare. I know you were drunk and it's ok, things happen. Don't worry, everything will be alright. We can go back to being friends like we were and pretend last night didn't happen at all…"

She did not let me complete, "Ssshhhh…Quiet Aditya, please calm down. You don't owe me any explanation. But you also don't get to pretend last night didn't happen. A lot has happened. And I cannot forget about it. But leave it, that's my problem, not yours. For the record, it did not happen because I was drunk or I was out of my senses. I was full well in my senses, aware of every single moment. It happened because of what I feel for you. The alcohol only helped me get some courage to be able to tell about what I feel. I meant every word you heard yesterday. And you don't reciprocate my feelings, I get that; you don't have to. I assumed you might have left your past behind and moved on. But you haven't, you still love her with all your being. Go find her and get her back. You are still madly in love with her idiot!"

Tears rolled down from her eyes as she said that. "I know how much it hurts when you don't get your true love. I felt that just last night", she looked at me, and smiled through her tears.

"You are really special. I have never cried for a man, you are the first one. And don't think that I am not hurt. I am no great generous person, I am just as human as you are. But I love you and I want you to be happy. Your happiness lies with her. Just go Aditya and complete your life, complete yourself. Get her before it's too late."

I wiped her tears and kept my hand around her shoulders. She rested her head on my shoulder. She was still crying.

Suddenly she stood up. "No Aditya, don't give me your shoulder to cry. I might get habituated to it. I won't get your support, or care when you will be away from me. I don't want to regret it then. So just back off"

I stood up and went near her. She was looking away from me. I turned her towards me, "Listen Avantika, more than anything else, you as a friend are more important to me. You had said once that people come and go, but some people always stay with us in our heart. You are one of those few people who get to stay in my heart, Avantika. And don't forget I will always be there for you. You can always have my shoulder to cry on, not that I want you to cry, ever. I will never let you fall. I am there with you in every phase of your life - good or bad. So what if I don't reciprocate your feelings? You are still my best friend. We are not bound to each other, and yet we don't feel the need to go away. You are a true friend. And you might have not got your love, but you still have a true friend"

She hugged me tight. Our friendship got stronger after this day. Girls like Avantika must be rare, I wouldn't imagine a lot of women who would continue being friends with a guy they loved. We went to Dunkin Donuts to get some hot coffee, it was too cold outside.

"Avantika yesterday you were taking about your family. Is everything alright?"

"Just leave that topic Aditya. We will talk about it after some other day"

"No Avantika please tell me. May be I can help you"

"There is nothing you can do Aditya, leave it"

"Come on, it might make you feel better to talk about it"

"You know that day you were talking about passion. You had said that it is important that everyone be passionate about something in their life and have an aim to work for. Well, not everyone can achieve their aim, sometimes fate plays a cruel game"

"I feel that we are responsible for our destiny"

"No Aditya. destiny is its own master. I still remember, I was in 9th grade and Di was in 11th. Di had got 95% in her final exam. I had got 86%. 86% was not bad at all. All celebrated Di's success. No one even bothered to check my report card. I had got a trophy for my outstanding performance in Art, no one even bothered to see it. Like every time I was ignored. They treated me as if I did not exist. When my teacher used to praise me in front of my mom, do you know what my mom used to say, "What are you telling ma'am, what will she do if she is good in art? These are all useless fields. See her marks in math they are drastically less than her elder sister" When I was in 11th grade, there was this workshop on fashion photography I wanted to attend. I knew my parents would not allow me. Without telling anyone, I sneaked out of my house and went to the workshop at the outskirts on Delhi. When I returned home in the evening, my whole family was waiting to scold me. I tried to explain everything but nobody would listen to me. My father slapped me in front of everyone. I refused to break down and told everyone what I wanted to be in life. I told them I am not Di, who can study for 10hrs a day. I can never be like her. I told them I don't want to be an engineer or a doctor; I want to be a fashion photographer. That's my ambition. On this my father said, "What low-class dreams you have! Look at your sister, she secured an admission at the Harvard University, and look at yourself. What will we tell others that Dhanraj Shekhavat's daughter is going to be a fashion photographer?" My dream was low class and Di's dream was high class. My ambition, passion, dreams, everything was rejected. I never wished to come to MIT. I don't regret it now, otherwise I would never have met you. But then, it wasn't that I never had a passion in life either"

36

The Pact!

"I apologize for my harsh words the other day Avantika, and I wish I could take my words back. But it's still not the end of the world, if you are really so passionate about fashion photography, you can still pursue it"

"The same goes for you, you can still get Aditi back in your life, it's not the end of the world, you don't need to give up so soon"

"My case is different. It seems more like I am aiming for the Mission Impossible!"

"Do you think mine is as easy as ordering a donut at Dunkin's? Come on man, think about it. Someday, you will have fulfilled all your dreams, but you won't have Aditi with you, then what use would it be? Would you really be happy then? Don't let that happen, you can still save yourself that pain!"

"Avantika don't change the topic. We were discussing your problem"

"Ummm…Ok, let's do this. " Umm ok so lets do this, its a pact….." then, I will do whatever you want me to. You bring Aditi back and I will become a Fashion Photographer, if that's what you want!"

"Avantika, that's ridiculous! There is absolutely no connection between my relationship or the absence of it with Aditi and you pursuing fashion photography as a career"

"Scholar,. if you sort things out with Aditi and restart your relationship with her, I will have more faith in this world, believing miracles can happen, and impossible things can become possible. Your achievement, will give me the strength to take my dreams up! Don't you get it! It will give me strength and make happy to see you happy"

"If I agree to make that happen, you have to promise you will do what you just said"

"Yes I promise you that the day you will get back with Aditi, the same day I will apply for an admission in a college to pursue Fashion Photography"

"In that case, you might want to procure the necessary forms right now, you will need it"

"Oh, how I wait for that day!"

Earlier, it was just me dreaming and wishing Aditi to be there with me, and regretting her absence. Now I had an added motive to bring her back. Not only my dreams, but Avantika's dreams were also now connected to us. I was already responsible for the damaging Avantika's feelings, I didn't want to be the cause for destroying her dreams too. It would be too much to bear in life. She could have blamed me, yelled at me, held a grudge for doing what I had done to her, but she didn't. She had behaved very mature and taken it very coolly. But I realized that that didn't mean she didn't feel the pain. She was going through the same pain that I was. I am sure there would be tears in her eyes whenever she was alone. I was the guilty one to have brought about those tears.

Avantika continued to greet me with a smile, she continued being friendly and happy around me. But I could see the pain through her smile. Didn't I feel the same thing for Aditi?

Ever since Avantika and Alex had broken up with each other, I was getting torn apart trying to balance my time between both. Alex and Avantika refused to speak to each other, they were completely loggerheads with each other. I couldn't spend time with both of them together. So I had to spend half my day with Alex and the other half with Avantika, and it was taking a heavy toll on me. I felt it was time someone shook some sense into them and sorted out their problem. I decided that someone had to be me.

One day after our classes, I called them both in the Robert's garden which was one of the innumerable gardens of our campus. They were not at all pleased to see each other. I reached five minutes late, on purpose. Both of them would have been at each other's throats had I been a little more late.

"Hey guys!"

"Aditya, why have you called us here right now? We have other things to do!"

"Avantika calm down. Listen to me guys. And please don't interrupt me now" Avantika was about to say something, but I cut her short.

"Both of you were very clear from the day one of your relationship that you were just having a casual fling. Then why the hell are you being such enemies to each other? Our friendship was way stronger than your fling. Stop behaving like this. You both have said it at some point of time or other than you won't make it together beyond a year. Then why do we have to stop being friends together now? Stop being such angry people"

Silence.

"Well you have a point Aditya. We can still be friends, if Alex is ok with it?"

Alex agreed too. "Yes, you are right. Let's be the three musketeers again." he said with a smile, "Group hug time guys"

We all had a tight hug. This seemed a lot easier than I had imagined. I was really very happy. For the first time I had done something nice. For the first time I had resolved a problem. Generally I was the cause of the problem, and it definitely felt great to be at the other end.

It was the last Sunday before classes began regularly as per schedule again. I received Avantika's text early the next morning; she wanted to meet me at her apartment. I was worried, and asked her if everything was alright, to which she never replied. It only made me more worried, and I ran all the way to her apartment. I rang the bell, twice, thrice but she did not open the door. All I could hear was very loud music coming from the house. I rang the bell again, but no response. Finally, I called her up, "Avantika what is going on? I have been ringing the bell for the past half an hour and nobody is answering the door. You woke me all worried if everything was alright…"

She opened the door. "Sorry, I could not hear the bell over the music"

"Avantika what was so urgent that you needed me here at this unearthly hour? This better be something important, I have sacrificed my sleep for you here that too on a Sunday!"

"Stop grumbling and complaining. Stop sulking. When you hear me out, you will feel it was worth it"

"So what is it after all?"

"Patience son, patience!" saying that she went into her room, and I followed her inside.

"Avantika, I am in no mood for any kind of pranks right now. I am damm sleepy man"

She took out a flight ticket from an envelope. There were two tickets actually. One was from Cambridge to Mumbai and the other was from Mumbai to Vadodara.

"Avantika what is this?"

"They are plane tickets duffer, can't you see?"

"I can see it. But for what?"

"You forgot so soon? If you manage to resume your relationship with Aditi, I am going to pursue fashion photography as a career. We had a deal. So I could not wait to achieve my dream"

"Avantika, you want me to go to India, like now? How can I go to India now? This is not the right time"

"Believe me this is the right time. In fact this is the perfect time. I want you to celebrate your birthday with her."

My ears picked up the word birthday. Then I remembered that my birthday was fast approaching. "I just forgot it was going to be my birthday soon"

"But how could I forget that on 26th December a creature like you was born! So hurry up. Pack your bags. You don't have much time. You have to catch a flight at 7:30 today"

"But...What about college?"

"Don't worry I have planned everything. I have your leave application ready with me. It says you have a medical emergency at home. I deliberately told you about this at the last minute so you would not get a chance to back off and the college authorities would also not get suspicious"

"What about studies, all those classes I will miss?"

"Don't worry scholar. Today is a Sunday so it's a holiday. Then you have to only miss two days of college that is 21st and 22nd I will share my notes with you and explain everything you wouldn't understand, which I am pretty sure would be nothing. Then 23rd, 24th, 25th, 26th and 27th are holidays due to Christmas. College begins on 28th. Your return flight is on 27th midnight. So go, celebrate your birthday with Aditi and be back in MIT on the eve of 28th, just in time for classes to begin the next morning. Am I not brilliant?"

Silence. I am trying to grasp everything that she just said.

"Really Avnantika, I must say I am glad to have a friend like you. People like you are hard to find. I mean you sacrificed your love, for your love. You are letting me go to the person whom I love just to see a smile on my face, just to see me happy. You are seriously one in a million"

I hugged her tightly. I did not want to leave her. There were tears in my eyes. I was happy but at the same time I was sad for Avantika.

"I know!" she said hugging me back. "Enough of this melodrama. Don't think that with all this I will forgive you! I am not leaving you so easily Aditya Patel. You will have to pay for this."

I packed my bags as quickly as I could. I was so excited. Finally I would meet Aditi. I was so, so happy. In no time I was all set to go.

I thought in my mind, "Aditi, I am coming"

I finished all the formalities with the college and Avantika accompanied me to the airport. "Go and complete your life"

"You keep your admission form ready"

"Yes sure, I would love to. You take care and call me as soon as you reach"

"Of course! Bye!"

"Bye!"

37

From where it all started...

I reached Vadodara the next day. I was back in my city, in my home, in my territory. The feeling was beyond words. New things fascinate us but the old ones make us smile. My face lit up when I saw the streets I had seen all my life so far, the vegetable vendors sitting on the roads, the endless traffic, the buffalos and cows coming in the middle and lots more. I wanted to visit Aditi even before I met mom or anybody else. After our separation only Nandini Di had been in touch with her. The last update that I had about her was that she had made it to a government college, just as she had wanted and was studying computer engineering. I knew nothing beyond that.

I reached her house only to find it locked. All the memories from the past came flooding back to my mind - the night on the terrace, her birthday gift, our first kiss, how I helped her to arrange everything, and so many more.

Mr. Desai, my old enemy was standing out. "Sir do you know where Aditi has gone?"

"How do I know, she is your girlfriend!"

He hadn't got over that afternoon when I had given him a piece of my mind for doubting Aditi's character and insulting her. I was disappointed, and it was pretty evident I was.

A little while later Mr. Desai spoke up, "Her uncle and aunt took her back home. She must be staying with them. I don't know more than that"

"Thanks a lot uncle"

I got worried the moment I heard that. I didn't even an ounce of faith in Aditi's uncle and aunt, especially her aunt. She could do anything. I tried calling Aditi on her old number, but the system said that the number did not exist. I couldn't meet mom when I was so worried and depressed, I wouldn't have any answers to the questions she would shower me with.

Mom had moved in with Raghu uncle and she was keeping much better now. Her panic attacks had lessened. I decided to meet Aditi first, and then go to mom.

I had no idea where Aditi's uncle and aunt lived. Aditi had changed her number. I called Nandini di, but she also did not have any idea about where was staying these days, nor did she have her latest phone number.

I realized I was hungry and went to the old coffee shop near the school where Aditi and I would get together to study. I was walking down the memory lane again and ordered her favorite chocolate brownie.

I looked around. Nothing was changed. I took a corner table, so I could absorb the entire view of the shop.

A tall girl with beautiful eyes, in an beige kurti entered the coffee shop. It was Aditi! My heart skipped a beat. I did not know how to react. All these days, I had been practicing my lines of what I would say to her when I met her. Now when I saw her in reality, I was dumbfounded.

A tall, handsome guy came up behind her and put his arm around her shoulder. My heart sank. I could not believe my eyes. I was shattered, all over again. Aditi saw me. Our eyes met. She was stood motionless and I was shocked and surprised seeing her with this guy. I did not know what to do. They sat on the table just in front of mine.

Aditi sat down facing me and the guy with her sat opposite her, with his back to me. I was disappointed and angry.

How could she do this to me? How could she give me so much pain? I had said no to a girl like Avantika for a girl like her! How could she have moved on so quickly? Because of her I had left everything, just to see her once. I could not believe myself that for her I had fought with mom, I had left her alone suffering in the hospital for a whole night! I had been so rude to my mom for this girl! I had believed in Aditi more than I believed in myself.

Was everything she said she had felt for me so fake or so weak that she could rip it apart and move on so quickly? She used to say that the whole world is fake but in reality she herself was fake. That guy was holding her hand, hugging her, feeding her the brownie but she did not say anything. And just months ago, she was doing those same things with me!

I could not see this anymore. I stood up to leave the café. Just as I got up, the glass of water in her hand shattered and fell off. The guy with her got really concerned about what had happened and if she had got hurt with the glass. I went towards their table on my way out, picked up the pieces of glasses and gave them to the waiter who had rushed to clean up.

"Thanks a lot bro. I don't know how it fell from her hand" the guy with Aditi was telling me.

"Don't get surprised, she has a habit of breaking things, am I not right Aditi?"

"Do you know each other?"

Little did he realize that we not only knew each other but there was lot more between us than that. But it was all now broken into pieces like the pieces of the glasses that I just picked up.

"Yes, we were in school together"

"Oh nice to meet you. What's your name?"

"Aditya Patel. How about you?"

"I am Abhinav Joshi Aditi's fiancé"

I was in for a shock. I was really very angry on Aditi. I could not believe that she had done this to me. Now I wish I had not come to India. Aditi had played with my emotions, and she had no right to do that. I wondered how long had they been together, had Aditi lied to me all the time?.

"Aditi, you did not call him in the engagement?", he asked Aditi, and then turned towards me, "We are getting married in four years after she completes her engineering. I expected a little more happiness for us mate, you seem disheveled! You alright?"

"Oh yes, congratulations. And, I should make a move. I just remembered I have to be somewhere important"

Before anybody could say anything more I literally ran on my way out. I took an auto to my house. Mom didn't stay there anymore. I unlocked it. I got nostalgic seeing everything around me. I went into my room and then to the terrace. I could not remember anything else but the first time Aditi had come to the house. Tears started rolling down my checks as I held on to the grill on the wall there. I cried and cried, shamelessly. There was nobody to see me here, and I didn't care even if there was someone. I had failed, I had failed in everything. Because of her I had neglected mom. I did not know how I could face mom ever again. I had lost Aditi, I had lost my life, I had lost everything. I cursed myself for getting into Avantika's ideas and coming down here and moreover, holding Avantika's dreams at stake for this, It would have been so much better if I would have remained unknown from this fact.

On the other hand, it was better to know the truth instead of being in dark. I asked the airline to shift me to an earlier return flight back to Cambridge. They moved me up for the next day. I decided to meet mom before I returned, I felt guilty for the way I had treated mom for the sake of a woman who could forget things and change men so easily. I had no idea what I would tell mom as to what I was doing here in India. I decided to think about it when I came to it. I took out my old bike, kicked and kicked and kicked it and finally managed to start it. I drove out to Raghu uncle's house.

38

Giving unexpectedly

I rang the bell. Raghu uncle opened the door.

"Aditya! What are you doing here? What a pleasant surprise! Falguni, oh Falguni! See who has come!"

"What is it Raghu, why are you shouting…Aditya, what are you doing here? Is everything alright? Your eyes look swollen. Have you been crying? Are you not sleeping properly?"

"Mom, breathe! At least let me come in! I was not crying. I am not able to sleep on planed, and so I had a sleepless night on the plane, last night"

"But is everything alright? Are your classes not going on right now?"

"Mom everything is fine, don't worry. My midterm examinations just ended, and I decided to take a break and come and meet you. I was missing you a lot and college was closing down for Christmas."

Anybody who would have looked at me would have figured out what a wreck I was. But you gotta say what you gotta say, even if it is a lie

"That's nice Adi but you should concentrate on your studies. You can call me when you are missing me, you don't just fly out here like that!"

"Don't worry mom I am here just for the day, I have my return flight tonight"

"You came here just for a day!"

She wanted me to focus on my studies and not 'just fly out here like that', but she was disappointed that I was here only for a day. I still don't know what I should do then!

"Sorry mom I could not get more leaves from the college. The flight was really tiring, I am still having the jetlag. Could I rest for sometime"

"Of course you can son, I will prepare your favorite dishes for you. You can have them for lunch when you wake up"

I lay down on the bed. The scene in the coffee shop kept replying in my head and it freaked me out. I felt guilty to have shattered Avantika's dream, while my own dreams lay shattered beyond repair.

It was time to fly back, and I bid farewell to Vadodara again. Yesterday, I was all excited on having landed in the city, and now I was going back wishing I hadn't come at all. I felt defeated, besieged.

I reached at 6 in the evening on Christmas day. It would have been 3:30 in the morning of the 26th in India. My birthday had already begun.

I took a cab straight to Avantika's. I rang the bell, she opened the door and was dumbfounded to see me.

"I was just destined to celebrate my birthday with Alex and you" I told her as she let me in. We sat on the sofa and I narrated the whole story.

"Aditya, fate played a cruel game with you. Maybe Aditi was just not destined to be your life partner. Maybe life has something better in store for you. But why didn't you talk to Aditi once. You should have tried to get her end of the story as well"

"Avantika what would I talk to her about? Should I have asked her what her fiancé does for a living? Or should I tell her how handsome he was? What could I talk to her? She left nothing to say!"

It only made me angrier to think about it all.

"You know what I will do for the rest of the days till college start again?"

"Tell me fast"

"When you had told me about your dream, I took your portfolio from your cupboard one day when I was here with you, and sent it to the California University of Arts. They really liked your portfolio and have offered you an admission there. Now there is just one small interview between you and your dream. The day before you sent me to India, I had received the letter of confirmation from them. While In India, I went to Delhi on my way, and visited your parents. I showed them the letter from the University and told them that the best Fashion Institute of the world was calling your daughter to learn from them. I explained how you were so passionate about it, I told them how you wanted your life to be. They were really impressed by the letter and they understood. It took some effort, but they understood. I told them how much you respected them, so you had not argued and kept your dreams aside to do their bidding. I was eventually able to convince them. I also told…" without letting me complete she hugged me and started crying.

"Aditya how should I thank you. I don't know how I will ever pay you back for this"

"Hey stop. You don't have to pay me back for anything. You have done a lot just being my friend"

Avantika's phone rang, it was her father. In these six to seven months, it was the first time that her father called. Everything was finally sorted in her life. I had finally done something good for her.

39

Incomplete Present

<u>*Starbucks, Near MIT, Cambridge, MA,*
United States of America.</u>

"Then?" I said taking a sip of coffee.

"Then what? Nothing!"

"Nothing? Nothing at all? This story sounds so incomplete!"

"That's all there is in my story. Nothing happened beyond that"

"Come on, this cannot be the end. You never looked back? You never tried to change things? She never called you or tried to talk to you?"

"Nope. Never"

"So how long ago did all this happen?"

"Two and a half years ago. Now I am in my final year at MIT"

"So what about Avantika and you?"

"I never felt the same way about Avantika the way she felt about me. I could not reciprocate her feelings. Just because I couldn't have Aditi in my life, didn't mean I would go for Avantika then"

"And as friends?"

"Avantika and I are still the thickest of friends. That is something that won't change ever. She is happy chasing her dreams and I am happy for her"

"And how do you feel about yourself? Are you happy with yourself?"

"Well, I could say I am learning to be happy"

"Aditya I don't know why I have a feeling that one day your incomplete story will get a happy ending. Someday everything will fall into place and you will understand everything clearly"

"It doesn't really matter anymore"

"No Aditya, destiny plays its own games by its own rules. You couldn't spend all your life by yourself any ways"

"I feel secure when I am alone, there is no fear of someone coming too close that the person is able to hurt you. I don't believe in fate, luck and destiny anymore either"

"You waited really long, a little longer couldn't hurt. Hang in there buddy, you never know when the tables would turn. True love won't just vanish!"

"Oh how I wish!"

"Life is too long to brood and sulk over the past. Life throws curveballs at us and we learn to deal with it. We may not understand why some things happen, but someday in the future all the pieces of the puzzle fall into place and bigger picture becomes clearer. Just hang in there, don't lose hope. And here comes my sister, so I gotta go mate. It was great talking to you. Think about what I just said!"

"Sure! And the next time we meet, I will pay back your twenty five cents"

"Hope to see you soon and listen to your 'happily ever after' saga"

40

Searching peace

Until yesterday, I was clear about the direction of my life. Finally I was beginning to get over Aditi and focusing on what was important. And then along comes the writer, one meeting with her and I am back to my lost self. She touched me where I was my vulnerable worst and provoked thoughts that I had long buried in the dark reaches of my head.

Aditi had clearly moved on, she would marry her fiancé once she completed her graduation. There was apparently no hidden truth in this, there was nothing to understand or dwell over on this.

I couldn't deny that I was still confused as to how Aditi did this to me. But maybe, she never meant any of what she ever said to me. Maybe she was lying all along and I got carried away. I refused to speculate and break my head over it. I wanted peace now.

I never realized when four years had flown past. After Avantika left MIT for California University of Arts, MIT had become boring for me. I would spend most of my time with Alex. But it was no fun, it was hard to kill time. Most of the time Alex would be busy with his girlfriends, and I would be left out all alone. I had nobody to share my feelings with. Talking to mom about things was out of question, she was not supposed to take any stress. I could talk to Nandini di, but I didn't have the heart to disturb her, she was happily married after all. Avantika was busy in her new world too, I didn't want to disturb her either.

I felt lonely. I still missed Aditi, but I tried to keep myself distracted enough not to dwell upon it much. I longed to go back to Vadodara, I missed my home town and the streets and the people there.

My stint at MIT was about to end but I wasn't sad about it. I wouldn't be sad to leave the US and go back to my country. Rather, I was happy. I was hoping my loneliness would come to an end once I was back in India. My stint at MIT was not quite how I had dreamt of it. Once in Vadodara I would have mom around and my cousins around, so no more being lonely.

I was one of the best students at MIT and this helped me bag a great job offer during the placements. I had bagged an offer at Thermo Fisher. It entailed two years of training, learning from my seniors, observing them keenly and gaining as much knowledge as I could. The next three years I would hold the title of a Jr. Engineer. I would be converted to a full-time permanent employee after serving five years at the company. I had to develop concepts and support development of electro-mechanical assemblies for laboratory equipment as part of my job, and apply the knowledge of materials and manufacturing processes to provide effective solutions to design challenges. I would also be required to develop and document mechanical designs using CAD tools and Pro/Engineer.

My graduation day was on the 15th of May. My entire family was super excited about it. They all were so proud of me and I was equally excited to see them. I had finally fulfilled my dream I had slogged like hell for it, I had paid my own price for it, but I had done it, and I was in a way proud of myself.

When I stood on the stage receiving the degree, I could see the pride in my mom's eyes. It was an extremely emotional moment for her. She was smiling and fighting back tears. She stood up and applauded my achievement.

She was one of the major reasons I chose to become an engineer, I didn't do it only for myself. I knew this would make her proud.

I was expected to report to work at Thermo Fisher in December, till then I had a long, long break with nothing to do.

Natasha was getting married at the end of the month. The past four years had distanced me from Ayesha, Natasha, Rony, Aarav bhaiya, Sanket, Sumit. I had been absent from all family functions, get togethers, birthday parties, etc. They would be really angry with me and take me to task once I was back. Natasha was just two years elder to me, and now she was getting married, it was an overwhelming feeling. She had been more a friend than an elder sister but I had lost touch with all of them, and I really missed them a lot. Ayesha and Natasha had sent me rakhis and letters every Rakshabandhan. I would send back the gifts for them and respond to their letters. But we did not talk much for the rest of the year. One broken relationship had affected so many other relationships in my life. It wasn't too late still, I could still make up for my mistakes. I decided to reach vadodara as early as I could and help out with the preparations for Natasha's wedding and in the process bond up again with all my cousins. Mom and I returned to India on the evening of the graduation day itself.

41

Back to where I belong

It was a great feeling to be back In Vadodara, I felt so relieved and relaxed with no more pressure of the studies on me. The first thing I did was visit my house. It had been four years since I had been there, and those four years had taken its own toll on the house. It was covered with thick layers of dust and cobwebs all around. I spent the day cleaning and scrubbing it, trying to bring it back to its old glory. I called mom in the evening and suggested that now that I had returned back to India, we could move back to our house. Mom agreed and I asked her to pack her stuff. I went to visit Natasha while mom was packing.

I rang the doorbell at Natasha's place. For a while there was no response, but there was a lot of in there. About five minutes later, Natasha opened the door, "Oh my God! I cannot believe my eyes. Rony, Aarav, Ayesha, Sanket, Sumit come out and see who's here!"

"What a pleasant surprise bhaiya! We never thought you would make it so early!", Ayesha hugged me as she said this.

I came in and we all went to Natasha's room.

"Good to see you bro! You have seriously surprised us" Aarav bhaiya said with the permanent intense look on his face.

"Well you all have also surprised me. I did not expect all of you to be here" That was a lie, I knew I would find all of them there. There was no other place any of them would have been then.

"We are not like you who forget their cousins" Rony said angrily.

"Oh so my little brother is angry!"

"Of course I am. I mean four years, not a single call not even a message. What is this bhaiya! You did not even wish me on my birthdays!"

"You could have called me too, you too have a phone, right?"

"Bhaiya, don't act smart. I called you on your birthday. Don't you remember?"

"Yes, but you should have called more frequently!"

"Oh please don't expect so much. You are the one employed at the MNC, I can't afford frequent ISD calls"

We had lost touch with each other, but we were up-to-date with the happenings in everyone's lives.

"Well I can at least afford an awesome branded watch for you" I fetched out the expensive watch I had bought for Rony. He had wanted it since years.

"I had lost all hopes about this one. Adi bhaiya you are the bestest!"

"You should never lose hope"

"Bhaiya that's not fair, why does only Rony get a gift! Why nothing for us?"

"Yes we all are also angry on you!"

Sanket and Sumit stood up from the bed and began protesting.

"Calm down everyone. I have gifts for everyone!"

As I said that, all of them jumped on me and started taking away and unwrapping and admiring their gifts. They were really very happy.

"So at last you got time for us! Now promise me you are not going anywhere till my wedding. You have any idea how much we missed you!" Natasha said hugging me.

"I promise, I am not going anywhere now" As I said this everyone came over and we had a group hug. They had really missed me, I could feel that. I felt bad that I had never thought much about anybody in my family for the sake of a girl for whom I ceased to exist overnight. I was grateful to have such lovely people in my life who loved me, cared for me, who celebrated my presence and were disappointed in my absence. How could I disconnect from such awesome folks for a girl who never reciprocated my feelings and who never understood what she meant to me. I promised myself I would never do that to them again. I would spend time with them and be there for them.

After lunch I had a talk with Rajesh uncle, Natasha's father and my father's brother about the arrangements for the wedding.

"Uncle what about the wedding hall and everything? Is it booked?"

"No Adi, actually everything was finalized so quickly that no wedding hall in our budget was vacant at such a short notice. Instead, we took a good banquet hall for the wedding"

"That's a great idea uncle. The hall would then manage everything from the décor to the food, and it would be a lot easier and better for us"

"Yes, that's why I am considerably relaxed"

"By the way which hotel have you decided?" "Welcome Hotel. They are well known for their arrangements"

"I agree uncle, it is a great hotel. So have you talked to them?"

"Yes, they have agreed. All the bookings are done."

"Superb! Is there anything I could help with?"

"Yes, the main task is still pending. We have to distribute the wedding cards. We are still just half way though it"

"Don't worry about that I could help you here. Give me half of the wedding cards. I will go personally and give them out"

"That will be a great help beta. Thanks a lot!"

"Oh come on uncle, Natasha is my sister. As a brother I am just doing my responsibility"

Rony and I took off to distribute the card, it was almost 8:00pm when we returned. As we all were together after such a long time we decided to go out and have dinner. I called mom and let her know about it. I had great fun with them. After a long time I had laughed freely.

We decided to have a night out at Natasha's place itself. Slowly everyone's secrets were coming out. We came to know about Rony's recent girlfriend. Sumit told us about his crush. Ayesha told that she had bunked her classes and had gone for a movie. Natasha showed me her to-be-husbands profile. His name was Himanshu Gandhi. He was quite handsome. He was an affluent chartered accountant. I was really happy for her.

"He is nice but not as handsome as me!" "Shut up Adi! At least he will not forget me like you!"

I knew I had to listen to those taunts and I was fully prepared for them.

Rony was looking suspiciously towards me. I was sure that now it was my turn to give out some secrets.

"What? Why are you looking at me like this?"

"Nothing I was just wondering with what kept you busy these four years!"

"I was studying, MIT ain't easy, you know"

"Oh really! Ok then tell me something about MIT. How did you find it? You enjoyed there?"

"Well frankly I was really lonely there. I missed you guys a lot"

These words were directly coming from my heart and I said it as convincingly as I actually felt them.

"Why you did not make friends there?"

"I made but..." "But what? Don't lie ha bhaiya. We have seen your pics on FB with a girl. What was her name? I guess it was starting with A" Our frequent FB user Sanket told everyone.

"Avanika, Avantika Shekhawat."

"Oh this Avantika seems to be interesting! Who is she?"

I told them everything about Avantika and Alex.

We were all sleepy by the time my story ended. We decided to call it a day and all went to bed.

42

Destiny decides the destination

The next day we were all surprised to see Nandini Di with us. She had flown down from the US to be with us for the wedding and help out with the arrangements. I was so happy to see her.

"Adi how are you? Have you got over everything? Back on track with your life?"

"Yes Di, I am totally over it. And after seeing you there would be no way I would not be good!" I hugged her as I said that. It was just another encrypted conversation we were having.

We were all together now and ready for a blast. We were all going to have a lot of fun and memorable times at Natasha's wedding. I had been distracted and missed all the fun in Nandini Di's wedding but this time there was no way I would miss it. I was going to enjoy like I hadn't in a long, long time.

Sangeet ceremony was so much fun. All of us cousins danced on the song *"Waah waah Ramji, Jodi kya banai!"* from the popular Hindi movie 'Hum Aapke Hain Kaun'. And then Nandini di and I danced on the song *"Dilliwali Girlfriend"*, from the first movie Aditi and I had gone to see together – 'yeh Jawani Hai Deewani'. When finally the DJ started playing, we all went crazy and danced like there was no tomorrow. We set the floor on fire and even made Natasha and Himanshu jiju dance together. I could not recall when was the last time I had so much fun.

Finally, it was the day of the wedding. As it always happen, everyone was busy with the last minute preparations. Last minute preparations are the inevitable evil of every event, no matter how well you plan, there is always something that gets left for the last minute. Everyone was running here and there in search of something or the other, there was total chaos around.

Incidentally, there was another wedding happening in the hotel. So one whole floor was booked by the other family.

I had absolutely no idea which of the rooms in the hotel were booked by us, it had been Aarav bhaiya and Roney's department. The only thing I knew was that the numbering of the rooms began from 1000 here, which wasn't much to go by. I was in-charge of the decoration department, but the hotel had done a great job of decorating the entire venue, leaving me with nothing much to do except oversee what they were doing best. I had just sat behind and relaxed in the air conditioning which was a welcome relief from the merciless heat outside.

A while later Nandini di came running towards me and said, "Adi go quickly and give these bangles to Natasha. She forgot them with me, the baraat will be coming soon now"

"Ok Di, what's Natasha's room number?" "It's 2211"

I was on my way when mom came and gave me huge boxes of sweets, "Mom, What is this? I can't have so many sweets right now!"

"Adi, stop being an idiot. They are not for you. Go and keep them in Natasha's room"

"Oh ok, room number 2211, right?"

"No Adi, its 2122"

"Nandini Di told me…"

"She must have misunderstood it as both the numbers are similar. Now go fast"

As I was heading up to Natasha's room, Rajesh uncle stopped me and said, "Adi can you please go to Natasha's room and bring my mobile. I went to meet her and forgot it there itself"

"No problem uncle, I am headed there myself. Room number 2122, correct?"

"No beta its 2112"

"Are you sure uncle?"

"Yes of course!"

Three different people had given me three different room numbers as Natasha's room. What was I supposed to do now? I decided to try the room number mom had given, as her memory was generally the sharpest. Before anybody could confuse me anymore, I quickly made my way to room number 2122. I knocked the door but no one opened. I tried pushing the door and it was unlocked. I could not see anything from behind the sweet boxes I was holding.

I went in and kept the boxes to one side of the room and said, "Natasha, get ready quickly. Your baraat should be here soon and…."

I stopped mid-sentence when I looked up and saw the bride wearing an intricate gorgeous red lehenga. My eyes could not stop looking at her. She was not Natasha. I was surprised. It was not Natasha, it was Aditi standing there.

I had imagined her as a bride a thousand times, but in the past four years I had left all hope and didn't believe I would ever get to see her like this. Why was she doing this to me? I wanted to tell her to stop making my life any more of a living Hell than it already was. But I was still ready to forgive her and spend the rest of my life with her, if only she would tell me what happened and meet me half way there.

I stopped myself from being any more stupid than I had been once. She was looking at me all teary-eyed. I could see that she still loved me, she felt it, but she didn't say a word.

We both stood there looking at each other, not saying a word.

"My mom is doing the last minute preparations. My whole family is running here and there, all excited. Go down and you will see all happy faces. You are dressed so beautifully as a bride. It is just as I had imagined for us. But if memory serves, you did not like red. You told me so yourself. So I had always imagined you in a pink lehanga. Leave it, there are many more things that I imagined and you said, that turned out to be wrong. You are fake Aditi, and so is everything you said. Your love, care, emotions everything was a whim of my imagination, none of it was real"

I realized I had tears rolling down from my eyes.

"No Aditya, it isn't like that.."

"Oh really? So I am the one not getting it? Maybe I am not, actually you are right. The past four years were supposed to be the best years of my life, they were my dream. And all of it got ruined only and only because of you. Every day, every second, every moment I used to ask myself that what wrong did I do that you punished me like this. Where did I go wrong?"

"It's not your fault, you did nothing wrong, but the situations were…"

"Don't blame the situations Aditi. Do you have any idea from how I suffered? I spent all my days lost, trying to figure out where I had gone wrong, how I had made such a big mistake in understanding you! For four years I have lived with the burden of these questions. But now, finally, I am over all this. I have no energy left to keep up. I have realized that there is no meaning in discussing anything with you. I have tried it earlier but it does not work. So just leave it, may you have a happy married life"

Finally all the anger and resentment that had been pressed down inside me had come bursting out. For a moment I was worried somebody might have overheard me. I turned around to leave, as I leave I could hear Avantika in my head, always pushing me never to lose hope and reminding my promise to her I also recalled the words of the young writer I had met at starbucks not so long ago.

"I love you Aditya" I could barely hear it, but Aditi said it. I closed my eyes.

"I wish you could have said this earlier Aditi. I might have believed you then"

"Adi you have to believe me one last time. Please Adi if you have ever loved me then please listen to me"

It was only making me angrier to hear her say all this. I looked into her teary eyes and held her arms tightly. "What should I listen to Aditi? Can you give me my answers?"

"Yes Aditya, just give me a chance to explain"

I let her go. "Then tell me why did you leave me Aditi? Why did you put me through so much? Why that day you came to the hospital but not meet me?"

"Yes Aditya that day I came to the hospital to meet you and sort out our differences. I could understand that going to MIT was your dream and you feared losing me so you did not tell me. I know you felt guilty for what you had done. So I came to the hospital. But in the hospital, I overheard you and your mother's conversation. Because of me you could not reach her when she needed you the most. The whole night she was suffering but you were not beside her just because of me. And this was not the first time this had happened. You had neglected your mother so many times because of me, I had become the cause of so much disturbance in your relationship with your mother. And the future would be no different, you would come across numerous crossroads where you would have to choose between your mother and me. Things wouldn't change. We both had no one but you. You could not be with both and keep both happy at the same time. Your mother was battling depression I could not bear to give you any more pain than you already had. I know how it hurts to be drift away from family, I have been through it and I would never want you to go through the same pain"

"Aditi then do you think doing all saved me from any pain?"

"No Aditya but I was new in your life, I just thought it would be easier for you to forget me than to get away from your mom. I would never want that because of me you lost the most important person in your life. I was acting on my first thoughts and I realize that had I thought it over better, I might have responded differently to the situation. If I could, I would definitely undo what I have done. I know I was immature to take such a decision."

"Aditi you should have talked to me once. A lot of misunderstandings could have been avoided."

"There was no point in telling you all this at that time, you would never have understood it."

"Wouldn't my attention any which ways get divided someday when I would be married, irrespective of whether I married you or somebody else? Mom would have had to get habituated to it. I was doing my best to maintain a balance between mom and you, there was no need for your sacrifice!"

"I did not want to destroy another life"

"Are you mad or something…!!!"

I kept my hands on my head and sat on the bed. I did not know how to react. I was angry but I did not know on whom. I understood it was not Aditi's fault. We were both far from being mature enough to handle such situations.

"And why are you marrying that fool Abhinav?"

"There is also a long story behind it"

"I have all the time in the world… Go on…"

"My aunt and uncle claimed their right on my grandfather's house. Being his first sibling, he had the first right on the house. He wanted to sell the house to overcome a loss in business. I could not do anything to stop him. They were not ready to let me stay with them either. I did not know what to do, I had nowhere to go. Aunty told me that if I get married early she can allow me to stay in this house for some more time. I promised her that as soon as I get my degree I will get married. She still refused to believe me. She forced me to get engaged. So I had to do all this…"

"Aditi one phone call, one message and everything could have been sorted out. If only you had trusted me once the whole thing could have turned out so differently."

"I know Aditya I should have talked to you earlier. Situation, time, destiny nothing was on my side. Everything went against me"

I stood up. I took her hand in mine. After such a long time I could feel this soft, tender touch.

"Let it be Aditi. Let bygones be bygones. I don't want to discuss this ever again. We both have gone through the same pain. Life is not made up of years, months or days. It is made up of moments. And I want to live every moment of my life with you. The moments that have gone, are gone. Let them go. The moments which are yet to come, will come when they have to. I just know one thing, that at this very moment you are with me, my life is with me. If there is no Aditi, then there is no Aditya. So, would you like to cherish every moment of your life with this over- romantic, person with no sense of humor, who still promises you to make you laugh in every moment?"

"Yes, Aditya. I cannot live without you. Enough of all this. Now we will never leave each other. Why am I telling you this? You were always there waiting for me, it was I who left you"

"No, Aditi. It's just that I was 5 minutes early and you were 10 minutes late!"

We hugged tightly, as tight as we could. We did not want to separate. All the boundaries between us were broken in a moment. The differences, the pain, the questions everything vanished. Love had prevailed.

"I love you Aditya, let's go away from here, somewhere far, where there is no one around. The way I had imagined"

"No Aditi we can't just leave like that. There is still a lot more to complete"

We went to Aditi's uncle and aunty. "I love her." I said holding Aditi's hand tightly, "We also have no problem if the house is yours. My love is enough for her. We can live without a house but we cannot live without each other"

We both smiled at each other and walked away from there. I knew it was going to be very easy in convincing them as they were only interested in the property and not at all interested in Aditi's life.

"Abhinav I am really sorry. I should have told you about this before. But I did not have the guts. Please forgive me" Aditi told her fiancé Abhinav.

"Aditi it would have been so much better if you would have told all this earlier. Do you have any idea how much you have insulted me here today?"

"I know Abhinav. You can put the whole blame on me. Tell them that there is something wrong with me and you can't stand me. I am ready to take a hit on me. Aditya is what matters to me now, nothing else bothers me in this moment".

"Don't worry Aditi I am not as cruel as you take me to be. For saving my reputation, I will not ruin yours. I will talk to my parents and I am sure they will understand. You don't worry about that. But you also don't get to walk free, one day you will have to pay for this!" he said smiling at us.

"I am ready to do whatever it takes"

The final task was the most difficult one, to convince my mom. Natasha's wedding ceremony had already started. We had wasted a lot of time, we did not want to waste any more.

Mom was really shocked seeing Aditi. I explained each and everything to mom. It was obviously difficult for her to digest everything.

"Mom I told you the love between us will never die."

"Do you know Aditya it has been 22 years since I had got married to your father. Even after your father died, my love for him never died. I know better than you that love does not fade away with time"

"Mom...

"I should actually apologize to Aditi"

"No Aunty you don't have to apologize for anything. We just want you to be happy, and give us your blessings"

"If you two are happy, why would I object to anything", she turned to me and said, "Aditya, you should have told me what was going in your mind. You should have told me that you were suffering so much. You were so far from us. I thought you must have moved on. You kids think that we are your enemies. No, we are your friends, you just need to talk to us. How can I sort your problem if I don't know if you have a problem? Leave it now. Let's start afresh"

We all hugged together. I had learned many lessons by now. One of them was that communication is must in life. Life was much, much, much simpler than it seemed. We unnecessarily complicate it sometimes. We just need to sit tight, and eventually everything falls into place.

Epilogue

After 5 years.

On a sunny day, in the scorching heat of Vadodara I was waiting for my friends at a coffee shop. I sat down and decided to have a milkshake to beat the heat.

As I was waiting in the queue to place my order, I saw a couple entering the coffee shop. They stood behind me in the queue. I felt I had seen that boy somewhere not so long ago. He might have been too young at that time but I was unable to recall where I had seen him or who he was.

My bill amount was Rs. 65. I gave the cashier a 100rs note. The cashier did not have the change. I had one Rs. 50 note and all the remaining notes were of Rs. 100.

Suddenly the guy behind me gave me a familiar smile. He took out Rs. 15 from his wallet and gave it to the cashier.

"Hey I cannot take this I don't know you"

"Well some time back I also did not know a girl. Yet she gave me 25 cents. I am returning the same. And I am guessing, 25 cents are almost equal to rs. 15, right? So all accounts settled now!"

We both smiled at each other. How could I forget that guy who had told his whole life story?

"I told you I will return it to you" he said collecting his order. I took my order and stepped aside as others were waiting in the queue.

"Aditya? How could I forget you? Goodness! I am so, so, so sorry. It's been what, five years?"

"I think it's more than that!"

Aditi was as beautiful as Aditya had described.

"So it seems you finally got your lady love! I told you not to lose hope!"

"Yes seriously things are never what they seem to be. You inspired me to keep at it and find the truth"

"No Aditya it's your destiny that brought you here."

"That's there but had you not compelled me to think through everything again, I would never have thought about it all and given it another shot"

"And then, it was the strength of your love. You can't deny that"

Aditi was totally puzzled. She had no idea what was going on.

"Whats happening Adi? You two know each other?"

We all took a table, Aditya and I narrated the whole story of how we had met in Cambridge. They invited me to their wedding and I congratulated them. I sipped my milk shake as I realized love really exists and that it could make miracles happen.